CONTENTS

BIGFOOTS IN PARADISE

THE MUSHROOM HUNTER

I REMEMBER I grabbed the table first. Then I stood up and hung on to the swaying wall. I was thinking I should get into a doorway. I'd always heard a doorway would be better but hell, when it was swinging back and forth like that? The door flapping loose? I thought I could dive through it maybe. If I was closer. If I had good aim. Flat out onto the gravel. That would still be better than getting sandwiched by the second floor. Then I thought I should just get under the goddamn table, but by then it was over.

"That was—" I said, catching my breath, "that was a big one." I looked at Chundo across several spilled bags of mushrooms. My hair was standing on end, some sort of static charge. The hanging lights were swinging and flickering. Glasses had fallen off the shelf and smashed into those already in the dirty makeshift sink. A bookshelf came to rest. A radio that had been playing Love and Rockets lay broken on the floor.

"That?" Chundo said with a smirk. He had a shaved head, the tattoo of a dragon looking up out of his shirt. With the tip of a knife, he picked up what I'd recognize now as a candy cap. "That was just a hiccup from God, Barn."

He was right. There would be similar quakes all up and down the mountains that year, leading to the big one. The ridge of the Santa Cruz Mountains would shake itself again and again, like a dog after a bath. I'd get used to it. Sand volcanoes would bloom in the dirt roads. Electric charges would leap from our fingertips. There would be days when we all had auras and halos, flickering turquoise and violet. Some nights my cot would sway so much I'd dream I was below decks on an old ship, but after a week of tremors I'd just roll over and keep snoring.

A tattooed woman and a kid came in then. She was carrying another bag full of mushrooms. The kid was laughing and hooting, weaving back and forth like he was drunk. Sparks frizzled green across the hat he wore, a wide, homemade contraption that was all tinfoil and clothes hangers and ribbons, a half-collapsed, crash-landed blimp. His long hair crackled. The ends of it lifted out from under the hat, up toward the ceiling. The woman reached over and touched Chundo on the cheek, and a green spark cracked between them.

"Shit, Laurel!" Chundo said, and jumped back.

"Tag," Laurel said. "You're it. And watch your mouth." She turned to look at me. "You are?" She had tired pale eyes and dyed red hair cut short, and she was wearing an old Smith's T-shirt cut to show her flat stomach and the piercing in her navel. Grapevines in black and green ink climbed up her arms and encircled her throat.

She was older than Chundo and I, somewhere in her early thirties. She took in my pink oxford shirt, the pressed creases in my jeans, the new sleeping bag rolled up by the door. When she turned back to Chundo, I saw Chinese lettering that I couldn't read low on her back. She was Chundo's usual type, except for the kid.

"Barnaby," I said. "Friend from high school."

She nodded over her shoulder, without looking at me. "Shit, Chundo," she said. "Who else is next?"

"Can I say that?" the kid said, studying the two of them. He turned to me. "Shit, Barnaby!" He had a big smile on his face, eyes jumping around to all of us. His hands fidgeted at the ends of his wrists, like they had somewhere else to go.

"I'm not sure that's a good idea," I said, glancing at Chundo, who rolled his eyes.

"It's another name for poop, Deke. Just say that." Laurel frowned.

"Poop, Barnaby!" He held out his hand.

"Poop, Deke," I said, shaking it carefully. He was no more than seven, and apparently some sort of terrible genius, I'd soon learn. In the light of the still-swinging lamps, his skin looked pale and luminous, the skin of a shining white ghost.

"He'll stay in the spare room," Chundo said. "Give it a freaking break, Laurel, and get him a beer."

Still frowning, Laurel reached into a portable cooler and handed me a bottle. I thanked her, but it didn't seem to help. Chundo opened her bag of mushrooms, poured them out on top of everything else on the table, and started sorting through them.

"People pay you for these?" I said. "Really?"

"Behold, the fruit of the mountains," Chundo said, holding a mushroom aloft. Deke giggled. "Wait till you see the one we're going for, the real prize. The One Mushroom to Rule Them All . . ."

Laurel rolled her head to the side. She looked exhausted. "OK, I'm out," she said to Chundo. "Keep a real eye on the beast this time, will you?"

"By the beast, she means me," said Deke.

Chundo sighed.

"Yes," Laurel said, not particularly kindly. "By beast I mean you." She lit a cigarette and walked out. She looked up at the sky and her shoulders relaxed.

"Watch this," Chundo said. He snapped his fingers at the kid like he would at a bartender. Deke grabbed a pair of welder's goggles from the counter. He scampered onto a stool near the stove and then pulled them down over his eyes.

"Ready!" he said to Chundo, giving him a thumbs-up.

Chundo held up a mushroom. It was long, white, and shaggy, like a beard.

Deke leaned in close, studying it. "*Hericium erinaceus*," he said, pronouncing it carefully. "Lion's mane."

"Not a *Hydnum*?"

Deke made a face. "Definitely not. It doesn't look anything like a Hydnum!"

"Good thing," Chundo said, nodding. "They taste like shit."

"Taste like shit," Deke repeated, nodding firmly.

Chundo held up a large orange one.

Deke rolled his head and sighed. "Chanterelle, of course," he said. "*Cantharellus cibarius.*"

Chundo held up another. He made it disappear and then reappear from behind Deke's ear.

"Porcini." Deke grinned.

"What's the Latin?"

Deke sat up straighter. "*Boletus edulis.*"

"Don't you mean edulatis?"

Deke frowned. "No such thing."

"No such thing. No such thing," Chundo mocked. "You know what being smart will get you, little beast? A mortgage. A day job. You got to dumb it down a little, mister. And lose the fucking hat."

Deke nodded seriously. "Dumb it down." But he put one hand on the brim of the hat.

Chundo snapped his fingers again. "OK, kid, get lost."

Deke climbed off the stool, but hovered closely while Chundo cooked. I did, too. For all his flaws, Chundo had always been a great chef. He diced the chanterelles and put them in a flat pan without anything else. He turned on the propane, lit the camp stove with a match, and water appeared from the mushrooms like magic, bubbling and hissing.

"Sweating them brings out the flavor," Deke whispered to me. "The water gets steamed out and all the stuff gets more concentrated." I couldn't see his eyes behind the goggles. In another pan, Chundo added wine, butter, garlic, cream. "The fats will add more flavor too, right, Chundo? Right, Chundo? So will the garlic."

Chundo didn't answer, but mouthed the kid's words back to me silently, mockingly, over the kid's head. "Deke, I said get bent."

Deke kept watching the pan. When the water had evaporated from the mushrooms, Chundo poured them into the wine mixture. He stirred it with a wooden spoon, and then grudgingly let Deke taste it. Deke nodded. Chundo added some black pepper and tossed the whole thing over spaghetti that had been draining in the jury-rigged sink. He poured it out onto two plates, clearing space on the table by pushing more mushrooms out of the way.

Chundo and I sat down. I looked at the kid. "Do you eat?"

"I eat," Deke said, in a fast whisper. "I eat mushrooms and noodles. I eat tofu but not tempeh, and fish if it's not halibut or smelt or Atlantic salmon, though the Pacific salmon is mostly OK because there's not as much fat in it. I do not eat lima beans or French fries or potato chips or cheese puffs."

"He'll eat later with his mom," Chundo said.

"Are you hungry?"

Deke pulled off the goggles and stared at my plate. "Kinda."

Chundo sighed loudly, but I cleared a spot next to me and poured a bunch from my plate into an empty bowl from the counter. Without a word, Deke climbed into a chair and dug in.

Hesitantly, I did too. They were my first real mushrooms outside of a can and they were pretty good. Rich, nutty, and firm, they concentrated the flavors of earth and tree the way oysters concentrate the flavors of sea.

After wolfing down the bowl, Deke broke out into hiccups. Chundo threw down his fork, exasperated, and pointed at the door. Deke slid out of the chair and headed out, head down. But on the way to the door he let out a particularly large gulp of air, and at the same time the ground shook again under our feet, a tiny tremor. Deke turned back to us, his hat on crooked and his eyes big as plates, his mouth a big O.

It was all of it. The craziness of the quakes, the crazy sparks, the strangeness of seeing Chundo again after so long. All the mushrooms everywhere, and the smells of dirt and garlic, eucalyptus and lavender and beer. The idea of Deke, of crazy Chundo with a kid. What was I thinking?

I laughed, choked on a piece of chanterelle, and snorted cream out of my nose. I spluttered and couldn't stop myself, even under Chundo's measuring, ironic eye.

Deke eyed us warily from the doorway. Then he claimed a goofy bow and darted out into the night.

«»

I'm not sure what made me think I could save Chundo from himself. It hadn't worked before. Chundo and I had been friends as boys in New Jersey, had hated each other in middle school, and then in high school we'd joined forces again and for a while we'd been inseparable. Unlike me, he'd been a brilliant student of physics, and several of our teachers thought he was headed straight to Stanford or Princeton, and from there to publication and teaching and tenure.

But I knew Chundo was too rough and tumble, too self-destructive for academia. He started up a band, the Whirling Pervishes, just before he dropped out, and they actually opened a few times for Phish and Robyn Hitchcock before they imploded. Their brilliant lyrics, the crazy, intricate harmonies: that was all Chundo.

We were a strange pair—I was the fat kid from the suburbs with Izod shirts and loafers. He was the wiry punk rocker, taking life by the throat and shaking it. I idolized him. And it worked, for a while. I followed Chundo from club to club. I bought drinks for everyone and, worse, made sure everyone had a good time. I paid for everything, at every club. When the last band broke up, I still tagged along dutifully with Chundo from girlfriend to girlfriend.

Finally, after his parents kicked him out, then his uncle, and then his sister, Chundo moved into our spare room. He spent time watching TV, eating our food, and having loud sex with a steady stream of tattooed girls in the afternoons.

My dad had never liked him, and when he found out that Chundo had pulled a knife on me when both of us were drunk, cutting me a little just under the ear, it was the last straw. Chundo was out on the street. I went to therapy.

Then, years later, I see his name on a poster in Santa Cruz. I think about it for a while. Despite my better judgment I call the club, and they give me his number. We get a beer. He's calmed down, he says, after some really bad years in Hoboken. The West Coast has been good for him. He apologizes for taking advantage of my dad and especially me. He's hunting mushrooms, he says, and selling them to high-end restaurants in Berkeley and Pebble Beach. Not a lot of money, but between that and the occasional gig as a studio musician it's enough to get by, he says unconvincingly.

Some nights, he says, he'll set up his guitar and amp on a ridge. He'll turn the volume up as high as it can go and sing old Johnny Cash and Hank Williams to the whole of Monterey Bay, which spreads out before him flat and silver and glowing with the captured light of the moon.

"Barnaby," he says, "you've got to let me show you. These mountains are God's country. There's no other place like it in the world."

He looks older than he should, ragged around the edges, but the spark is still there. He asks if I want to come join him for a while. He's on the trail of this rare mushroom, one that should bring in a lot of money. I should come along, like old times.

And then he asks if I'm going to pick up the check.

Despite that, the contagious enthusiasm is still impossible for me to resist, though I should have known better. It's the late summer of 1989. I'm twenty-seven and single again. Unlike the smarter guys who are designing circuit boards, getting machines to talk to each other, and starting companies, I'm living in my dad's California basement, doing occasional consulting work.

So I pack up the BMW with a sleeping bag and the new Mac Plus and cruise slowly up Highway 17. From the summit, I drive a succession of smaller dirt roads, through redwoods and scotch broom and brush until the hills swallow me.

«»

"It's a variant of the *Amanita*, Barnaby. Extremely rare. Extremely valuable," Chundo explained. He exhaled and passed me the hand-rolled cigarette with an expansive gesture, though I'd paid for the all-natural tobacco and the papers, too.

The smoke spiraled up through the branches of the redwoods. It was night. Late spring. I'd been there a week or two. The air was dry and tasted of eucalyptus and salt. There was no moon, really, but from where we sat out on the ridge you could see down the long hills to the lights of Santa Cruz and Watsonville, there on the water. The power plant in Moss Landing flashed its red lights. Out on the water, fishing boats shone spotlights across the surface to call up the squid. Deke was finally asleep in a sleeping bag on my lap—we'd hit it off when I showed him the games on the shiny new Mac.

"The beautifully elusive *Amanita ostriatus*, my friends," Chundo continued. "Imagine, brilliant green all over, all the way from the volva to the tip of the cap, not just the normal plain brown or pale yellow of your average Amanitas. A doctor in Oregon found a fruiting once, and he said it glowed brightly enough he could see it from ten feet away."

"Here?" Laurel asked, her pale eyebrows going up. "He found it down *here*?"

Chundo nodded. "Down here. Up here. They were deep in a grove of madrone, up on the side of a ridge facing the sea. He said the fruiting stretched for a square mile." He spread his hands. "Imagine, a fruiting bigger than you could see the ends of!"

"Like *Amanita* from Maaars," I said sagely, nodding like I knew what I was talking about. *"Maar*tian Aman*iii*ta," I pronounced, in my mock California surfer-dude voice. The wind caught the smoke and wrapped it around my face like a surgeon's mask.

Laurel said, "Are they edible?"

"Absolutely," Chundo said. "They're supposed to have the best flavor of all the Amanitas. Like Irish butter. This doctor even claimed the tea he made from the caps and stems cured his daughter's fever."

I snorted. Voice deep, like a movie trailer voice-over, I said: "Some say that it could even raise the dead."

Laurel frowned. Chundo laughed. I looked up. The moon was a thin fingernail of fire. The stars spun in tiny circles.

"Get this," Chundo said, "no one really believes it exists. But we are going to prove them wrong! And I'm betting Chez Panisse will be willing to make it worth our time if we do. Nepenthe, too."

"We are?" It was clear from Laurel's tone this was the first she'd heard of this. "I didn't think restaurants were brave enough to serve Amanitas."

But Chundo was fired up. He stood up and paced back and forth. "If we don't, who will?" The dragon on his neck grinned at us. "And they'll serve these, you watch. The flavor will be worth the risk. Late rains this year; it's probably just out there waiting for us. I mean, how many times do you get a chance to make history?"

"He's hard to argue with," I said to Laurel.

She rolled her eyes. "The rest of us seem to manage," she said, and then sighed. "Sorry, the little beast was particularly intense today."

Deke yawned, turned around on my lap, and reached for his hat. He seated it firmly on his head. "Does it have eggs, Chundo?" His voice was full of sleep. "The *Amanita*?"

"Mushrooms don't lay eggs," I said. "They're not chickens, little beast."

"Actually, these do have an egg form, kid," Chundo said, nodding at Deke. Deke's sleepy face lit up. "You can slice it from top to bottom and see the outline of the whole mushroom inside—the mushroom the *Amanita* will become."

"Like an embryo, I guess," I said.

"What's an embryo?" Deke looked up at me.

"Like a baby mushroom."

"It's not *like* a baby mushroom. It *is* a baby mushroom. It's got the cap and the gills and the stalk all in there, right, Chundo?"

"Inside every boy is the man he will become." Chundo nodded. "Of course, if we go out after it, it'll mean doing some deep hiking for the next few weeks. Might not be able to keep up with the cash crop . . ."

Laurel studied me in the dim light.

"There's the rent and all," Chundo said.

"It's OK," I said after a minute. "I can carry us for a little bit."

"The Chez will totally come through, Barn. And when it does . . ."

"It's all right," I said. I looked at Laurel. "It's OK."

She shook her head and looked away.

The bank of fog rolled uphill like an avalanche in reverse, wrapping us in a damp, eerie quiet. Chundo and Laurel hissed at each other, arguing quietly. They argued a lot. "Come on," I heard Chundo say. "Don't be that way."

I might have drifted off for a bit. I woke to Deke pressing his finger into my cheek. "I can see the future with my hat on," Deke whispered in my ear.

I nodded over-enthusiastically, the way you do with kids.

"No, really, I can," he said.

It was late. The fire was lower. Maybe it was a lack of sleep, but a shiver went up the back of my neck and my scalp crawled.

"Tell me something that happens in the future," I said.

"In the future," Deke said, "I am the best mushroom hunter in the whole state of California."

I could feel his warm breath on my face. "I bet you will be," I said.

"Like Chundo," he said.

We could see Chundo's silhouette moving around the fire, adding logs. "Like Chundo," I agreed. A small tremor wobbled the ground, but no one else seemed to notice. A tiny spark jumped from Deke's fingertip to mine. In the distance, three owls were calling to each other across the ridge. Chundo turned and cupped his hands around his mouth and called back to the owls, and one of them came in to check us out. It perched on a naked branch of madrone, just outside the shrinking circle of the fire.

"*Oooooh*," went the owl. "*Oooh-oooooh*."

"*Oooh*," said Chundo. "*Ooooooh-oh*."

"What are they saying?" I whispered to Deke.

But he was asleep again, his cheek pressing the hat into my chest. I watched as Chundo reached out his hand, and the owl came in to perch, sitting on his arm and studying him closely like an old friend.

Part of me was amazed, the part that was always amazed by Chundo. Part of me wondered if he was going to ask the owl for money, too.

« »

The next morning I took Deke into Santa Cruz and got gear. The kid *was* really intense, I'll give them that—just like the Chundo I remembered. Always talking. Always in motion. He was intensely interested in everything he saw, and it was as though his small head was so full of specifics he'd explode if he didn't let them all out. One day it had been the particulars of the ships that were used by the Romans when they invaded Britain in AD 43. Another time it had been the anatomy of sea urchins, how they had jaws and intestines just like people. He talked fast and low, details spilling out so close together it was hard to understand what ampullae were, exactly, and how they related to the bireme, which was evidently entirely unsuited to the waters of the English Channel. A creature? A ship? I didn't know. I liked it for the same reasons I'd liked Chundo as a kid. My dad had never been a talker, and without my mother our house had always been pretty quiet.

We got back close to lunch, and I could tell there had been a pretty bad argument while we were out. Chundo's face was cold and set, the way I'd seen it get before when things got bad. His eyes looked tired. Laurel looked like she'd been crying. Deke followed them around, telling them about all of the things we had bought, but both of them barked at him and sent him off. Subdued, he sat down with me to help get all the wrapping off of everything, to get the sleeping bags stuffed and tied on and the backpacks filled.

We locked up the shack and set out that afternoon along the ridgeline. Chundo had a specific search pattern, he said, that would take us back and forth across the wilderness areas. None of us could make much sense of it. Chundo walked up front, setting a hard pace. Laurel trailed along reluctantly in his wake.

At first Deke ran around between all of us, but he soon wilted in the heat, so I got him up on my shoulders and tried to keep up.

From the top of the ridge we could see from Monterey all the way up past Santa Cruz, the whole curve of the bay. Sailboats undulated just offshore, tacking and luffing. Whales rolled up and blew steam. Then we dropped down into a canyon that was thick with pin oak and madrone, going off trail. The deeper we got, the larger everything seemed—the trees were wider and incredibly tall. The plants loomed over us and blocked out the sun. I had the sense they were watching us as we trespassed deeper into unknown country.

We camped that first night beside a dry stream, in a cathedral of redwoods, a giant fairy ring. Deke and I cooked noodles. Chundo and Laurel drank vodka. They walked off into the gigantic trees and started arguing again, with Laurel's voice carrying over the hissing of the propane. I couldn't hear Chundo's replies, just his tone. It was something I'd heard a lot from him around previous women, always near the end of things.

"It doesn't bother me," Deke said. He was trying to catch a lizard that had emerged from a pile of rocks.

"What doesn't bother you?"

"I was reading your mind." He turned to me and pulled the welder's goggles off his face. His eyes were startlingly green in the shade of his hat. "Mom and Chundo."

"Oh," I said. I stirred the pot.

"They argue a lot, but I don't care."

The noodles were done. I turned off the stove, and suddenly we could hear Chundo's voice clearly. "Then give the fucking kid back so you can *get* a goddamn life!" he shouted.

"Maybe I will!" Laurel shouted back. "You asshole." She turned and stormed away into the woods.

Deke stared at me for a minute, and then put the goggles back on. His skin looked even paler.

"He's not my father," he said, quietly. He turned back to the lizard, which hadn't moved.

"Deke, you can't let . . ."

He reached out quick and grabbed the lizard. Holding it in his fist, he lifted it up to his eye level and studied it. "*Sceloporus graciosus*," he said. The lizard studied him back. "You're not either, you know," he said, as if he was talking to it.

I watched as Deke tightened his grip around the lizard. The set of his jaw reminded me of Chundo, that night when we'd told him to get out, or that night I'd tried to keep him from cutting himself after a girl had dumped him, and he'd cut me instead. Deke's face was expressionless. He squeezed the lizard and it struggled, whipping its tiny head back and forth and flailing a tiny arm.

"Deke," I said. "Dude. Step away from the lizard."

He looked at me. I shook my head.

"It's just a *Sceloporus*," he said, but he opened his fingers. The creature lay limp and seemingly lifeless on his small palm. "It's just a stupid lizard," he said, and tossed it back onto the rocks.

In the air, the lizard flipped, landed feet first, and ducked quickly into a crack.

Chundo yelled for Deke. And like I would have when I was younger, Deke jumped up, grabbed him a can of beer, and went running to his side.

« »

"We're getting close," Chundo claimed. The *ostriatus* would just be over the next rise, glowing green in the dim light of the woods, he was sure. He painted a brilliant picture of it, and even Laurel seemed to get caught up when he talked. It would just be one more short climb out of the brush, up toward the top of the ridge again. Once we got there, he said it would just be down in the next canyon, waiting by the stump of a redwood. Down where the fog would be keeping it damp.

We were four days out now, and in another one or two we'd have to turn back unless we wanted to live on mushrooms alone. Fires were burning over near Boulder Creek, and in the mornings our sleeping bags would be covered with a thin layer of ash. But the deeper we went into the backcountry, the more energy Chundo seemed to have. He began to look the way he always had on stage—leaping about, barking lyrics into the microphone, hammering on that old Ibanez. He powered up hills, his gaze skimming the landscape. He'd call out and gesture, and at first I'd see nothing but leaves and fallen branches. Then he'd pounce and conjure a large bouquet of *Craterellus cornucopioides* out of nowhere, like a magician pulling black flowers from a hat. He pointed out hidden beds of chanterelle, candy caps, milk caps, and even morels to me until I started getting the eye for them. We found chicken of the woods, logs full of oysters, old man's beard growing on the sides of slopes, sawtooths and slippery jacks, pink Russulas. They were from all different seasons, he said. We shouldn't have been finding them, and yet there they were. Deke's face glowed, rosy as the Russulas.

I remember thinking we were all of us small creatures, resting on the back of something immense and alive. I imagined all of those mushrooms stretching feelers out underground like broad subterranean creatures, white and blind, reaching out along the interconnected webs of tree roots that stretched for miles. Maybe they were all just different parts of one great, restlessly sleeping beast. Here were some black trumpets of ears, listening to the sound the wind made through the naked branches of the madrone. Here was the shaggy mane of a tongue, licking the salt out of the ocean fog. Thousands of little brown mushrooms were eyes watching the sea, the sky, the sun passing over. Watching us pass by, too, like faint stars caught on long-exposed film. I imagined I could sense its thoughts, even without Deke's hat. They were thoughts so slow moving and primitive that words to capture and convey them were useless. Language was nothing but the passing murmurs of ghosts.

That evening we set up camp on a low rise above the distant lights of a town that Laurel thought might be Corralitos.

Though we hadn't found the *ostriatus*, we had several pounds of other mushrooms. Using the little camp stove and the small set of knives I'd brought, we sliced them thin and dredged them in garlic. We dropped them into what was left of our olive oil and tossed in tiny pieces of bacon. We had chanterelle and oysters, black trumpets and candy caps and butter boletes. We had morels that were red, blue, and black, and a chicken of the woods that wasn't anything like a chicken.

Afterward, Chundo and Laurel sat next to each other on the ridge, not speaking. Deke was awake and quiet for once, and the air was full of static. We watched the auras flickering around us, blue-green, white, emerald—the colors of the sea. The sun went down and the October sky went purple and brooding scarlet from the fires. Stars exploded here and there in gaps between the roiling towers of smoke that streaked up and westward toward Japan, toward the burgeoning moon.

"I know it's out here," Chundo said, convincing himself. "We'll find it tomorrow, for sure."

Deke nodded sleepily, complete faith written across his face. Laurel wouldn't meet anyone's eyes. Chundo looked over at me. He looked old, then, and I realized that the Amanita was more than a mushroom.

Beneath us the mountain rumbled. The next morning, Laurel was gone.

« »

Her sleeping bag was empty and at first we thought she'd gone off somewhere to pee, but when she hadn't come back for an hour we started calling. From the rise we could see in all directions. There was no sign of her.

Deke looked pale and scared underneath that hat of his. Chundo looked even worse. He looked shocked, as though the idea of her not being there had never really occurred to him. The ends of his relationships had always been a surprise, always hit him hard, but Laurel's leaving seemed to hit him harder. This time he completely folded in on himself. He stood beside the stove for a long time, and his face took on that coldness, his jaw setting down into that angle that always made me wary. He looked smaller. The dragon tattoo seemed to bloat and fade.

Deke paced in circles around us, repeating the same questions, lifting up and checking under things. Where did she go? When did she leave? Where could she have gone? Could a mountain lion have taken her off? They were known to pull deer up into trees. Maybe she'd be up in a tree somewhere? Maybe we should look there? She's not under the sleeping bag. She's not on the other side of the hill? Then he stood in one place, shaking. He sat and pulled his hat down tight, clenching his face and trying to hear her thoughts.

Down by the tree line, I found something that was almost a trail. It led roughly downhill, off toward where the town might be. It was probably nothing more than a deer path, but Deke jumped up and ran down it at top speed, hands in the air, calling her. I yelled after him, but he either didn't hear or ignored me, and crashed headlong through the brush.

"We should get him," I said to Chundo, meaning he should go.

He looked at me strangely, as though I were a ghost. "What? Why?" He shrugged. "Maybe he'll find her."

"Maybe he won't."

He shrugged again, turned away, and started putting random things into his backpack. He looked up at the ocean and then down at his hands. "He's not mine, you know. She told me that."

I shook my head. "Look again. He *is* you, Chundo."

He didn't turn. I went down the path, and found Deke after half a mile, huddled on top of a charred redwood stump. His hat hung in shreds. His arms and legs were dirty and covered in welts. It looked like he'd fallen and split his lip. He watched me warily from behind his goggles.

"Come on," I said. I brushed him off. "We'll get Chundo and head back. She's probably gone back to the house."

"I'd know it if she was."

I knelt and looked at him. "Your hat's all broken," I said. "It might be hard to tell." I took his hat off and set it on the stump. When we got back to the camp, Chundo had packed up his things and was already heading down the far side of the hill, away from where we'd come.

"Chundo," I called. "Don't you think—"

He looked over my head. "I know we're close, Barn." He ran his fingers over his stubble. "I've got to finish this thing."

I studied him. I didn't actually think I knew the way back.

"Deke," Chundo said, snapping his fingers. "Let's go."

Deke looked up at me, and then back at Chundo. He didn't say anything for a minute. I couldn't read his expression. Then he let go of my hand, picked up his sleeping bag, and took it over to where Chundo was waiting. Chundo nodded. The two of them set off toward the next ridge.

I watched them go. Then I packed up the camp. There wasn't much, but it took me a long time. It took forever to pick the slugs off my sleeping bag and get the bag into the stuff sack. I considered packing Laurel's, too, but decided against it. There was a little bit of propane left, so I made coffee, and then there was a small tremor that sent ripples across the surface of the cup. A helicopter beat across the horizon, carrying a load of water toward where the smoke still billowed. I heard crashing in the brush and thought it might be a mountain lion, but it was only a squirrel chasing after two other squirrels. I imagined I could hear sounds coming up the canyon from the town. Car doors shutting, people and kids talking, laughing, and it sounded so clear to me—maybe it was a trick of the acoustics; maybe not.

Eventually, I stood up and went after them. Their trail wasn't hard to follow, down the steep side of the canyon and around a bend. Nearer to evening, I could see them in the distance sitting together, on the steep side of a hill beneath a cluster of oaks. When I got closer, I could see that they were eating, or at least Chundo was. Deke was staring down at something in his hand. Something green.

They watched me approach. "You came," Deke said. He looked like he'd been crying.

"What's wrong?" I said.

Chundo held up a green mushroom in his hand. "Nothing. We got it!" he said. His eyes were wide and had that manic stage gleam to them. He popped the mushroom into his mouth, chewed, and swallowed, and then reached down next to where he was sitting and pulled up another one. There was a large fruiting of them there, where he'd cleared away the leaves. He handed one to me. "They're delicious, Barn. Save them for The Chez though, OK?"

It was greenish-white, with a wide smooth cap and bright white gills underneath the head. It shone somewhat metallic in the late afternoon sun. It smelled like dirt to me, or maybe like a raw potato, just cut.

I looked over at Deke, who shook his head. "They're not *ostriatus*," he said. "*They're not!*"

"The legendary *Amanita ostriatus*!" Chundo said, frowning at Deke. "These taste incredible!" There was a tone in Chundo's voice I recognized. He was working hard to convince himself of something.

Deke looked back at the mushroom, and looked up at me again. He looked strange without the hat. Pale, like a capless mushroom himself. He whispered something I couldn't hear.

"No. Such. Thing," Chundo said, leaning over and poking Deke in the chest with each word. His voice had an edge now, and sparks were leaping from his fingers. I could see Deke wince.

"*Amanita phalloides*," Deke said again, a little louder. "Chundo, *don't!*"

"*Ostriatus*, kid. It's not a goddamn death cap. It's completely *ostriatus*. Do you see the partial veil on the stalk? The volva at the base? That's where the universal veil was when it was smaller. I found it, kid. Barn, I found it!"

Deke looked at me. I looked at the mushroom in his hand and shook my head. "Don't," I said. I was sure Deke was right. And I was sure that at least a part of Chundo knew it.

Deke looked back at Chundo, who was chewing aggressively and reaching out for more. Deke swallowed hard and sighed, and before I could say anything else he put the mushroom into his mouth and started to chew.

Chundo's eyes went wide, and he reached for Deke. And then with a terrible crash, both of them lofted into the air, as everything around us took flight.

«»

We might have saved him. We were four miles or so from the road to Corralitos. We might have gotten to a phone, to a hospital. But it was exactly 5:04 p.m., on October 17, 1989. I can pinpoint it so specifically now because that's when it hit, the big one that would be called the Loma Prieta quake. It brought down bridges and overpasses. It destroyed buildings and high-ways up and down the peninsula. It was televised as part of the warm-ups for the World Series in Oakland, and even the pilot in the Goodyear blimp said he could feel the shocks.

Santa Cruz is leveled. In the Santa Cruz Mountains, the epicenter, the force of an underground nuclear bomb whips giant redwoods back and forth like they're made of rubber. It pitches homes down into canyons, opens yawning crevasses, swallows highways. Aurorae like the northern lights fill the sky for weeks.

When I see him now at Funghi, his restaurant, Deke and I remember many things. I see the world spinning around me as the whole side of the mountain we're on liquefies. I see Deke cartwheeling in the air, his bright eyes open, his mouth that great O of amazement, his arms and legs spread wide, and chewed pieces of that mushroom are all around him, like tiny fish streaming out from his throat. Electricity crackles, and there are entire trees in the air, roots and all. Huge boulders hurtle by me, spinning off blue and white fire.

Deke says he remembers all of those mushrooms in the air, hundreds of them from all seasons spilling out of our back-packs and orbiting us. The glowing golden chanterelle. The bright red Boletes and Russulas. The blue-black Craterellus, like tiny trumpets singing out the end of the world. And yes, the green glow of *Amanita phalloides*, those death caps that we both know Chundo knew well.

Most of all, we remember Chundo. The sun across his brow, the half-moon below his feet, flying higher and farther than any of us, his arms stretched wide to embrace the sea. We remember how this man we both loved, despite our better judgment, took a giant step out across that horizon. And without a backward glance for us, how he was simply, terribly, gone.

CATCH THE AIR

For a long time, my father kept a vintage Travel Air in an old Quonset hangar on his family's old ranch. It was a beautiful open-cockpit biplane. He'd had it since he was a boy, when he gained recognition for being the first kid to fly solo across the Bering Strait. When I was a kid myself, I remember that he could live with it, out in that hangar, for weeks, along with his record player and his Scotch and the beat-up fiddle that was always his favorite. I'd have to bring him food. He'd blast his music, retool the strut assemblies, replace the vintage electronics, spread thin layer after layer of butyrate dope over the thin fabric wings. He would take that engine apart and put it back together by himself on a whim.

I remember the first time he took me up in that plane. I was six. He had just started teaching me to play that fiddle, and the fingers of my left hand were all sore. I sat in the front, with a headset that was too big and goggles that covered most of my face. I had to stretch up to see through the windshield. He had me put on the beat-up leather jacket, the one that smelled like whiskey.

"You ready, Gordie?" he said through the headset. I gave him a thumbs-up. He turned on the music—I'm betting it was Charlie Parker—and taxied down the rough little runway. He lifted us into the air. I felt my stomach drop.

"What do you want to see?" he asked.

I pushed the talk button. "I want to catch a cloud," I said. I held up a small spice bottle that I'd smuggled out of my mother's house that morning. Cumin—it still had some in the bottom.

"*Sí, sí.*" I heard him laugh through the static. "You got it, kid," he said.

He gunned the engine and took us higher. The air got cold. Clouds expanded, took on texture and detail, and filled up the sky.

"Deploy the trap!" he called.

I fumbled the top off and held the jar out. The plane banked right, and we dropped down into a wall of gray. Droplets of water condensed across my goggles. I pulled the jar back in and slapped the top on. Then I tucked it deep into the breast pocket of the jacket.

Then we flew across the South Bay, over fields of prunes being turned into rows of flat houses. We swung over the hangers at Moffett, where the Navy had once based blimps to patrol the coast. The music in my headphones soared and dipped, and we did too. We crossed the mountains and swung low over Monterey Bay. There were whales, at least ten of them, swimming north in a pod.

"Let me see it," my father said, after we landed. "Your cloud."

I'd forgotten about the jar. I took it out and held it up to the sun. Except for the leftover spice, it looked empty. I was close to tears. I handed it to him, and he held the bottle up toward the sun.

"Clouds are tricky fuckers," he said. He shook it, and held it up to his ear. "Hah! I thought so." He handed it back to me. "It's in there, all right. It's just gone invisible, to try and trick you into letting it out? Keep the lid on really tight, or maybe just open it up at night, really quick. You know, to smell it? But don't keep it open long, or *boom!*" He clapped his hands. The sound echoed from the walls of the hangar. "That sneaky *cabrón* will be gone in a heartbeat."

I had that bottle for a long time. I kept it by the side of my bed for years. After an intense dream I'd crack it open just a tiny bit. I'd hold it up to my nose until my heart stopped racing and I was tired again.

I did it so often that now I'll be sitting in a Mexican restaurant, or at a friend's house for chili, and the scent of cumin will bring it all back to me. The clouds. Those whales. That water.

And my father and I floating together up there over all of it, before any of his demons dragged him down.

≪≫

"How hard could it be?" Rory cursed over the radio. "It's just a big effing gas bag full of hot air. *I'm* a big gas bag full of hot air."

At another time, it might have been funny. His gut did hang out over those poorly appropriated hipster skinny jeans like a blimp hitched to a tall mast. And Rory was, well, Rory— an old friend of my father's, once a member of his band Old Dog Dreaming, and neither of them were short on personality. But we were going down fast and had other things to worry about. One of the cables that adjusted the breather valves was stuck letting out too much hot air, and by then we had drifted out over the water. A sailboat passed by the lighthouse and out into the waves. I could see the morning paddle-boarders down in the harbor, looking up at us wide-eyed.

Nikki and I swapped looks. Her red hair was damp with sweat. Her freckles sketched a crazy archipelago across the pale sea of her cheeks. If she wanted to be in charge, I was thinking, now was a good time to do something. But she shook her head: we both knew this was *my* problem. I kicked off my shoes, cut the gas, and handed her the burner control.

"Give me a minute," I said. "And when I hit the seat again, punch the igniter and give it a really big blast. Oh, and put that life jacket on." There was only one, I remembered. She nodded. I unclipped my harness and pulled myself around the hot burner and into the envelope, climbing up the struts embedded in the fabric walls like they were a ladder. It was about sixty feet high. My weight pushed the whole envelope over some, and the whole airship started to drift that way, but fuck it, if we went down into the water it wasn't going to matter much which side hit first.

When I got up to where the valve was, I ripped off a big piece of duct tape and slapped it over the hole. Then I slid back down, dodged the cowling around the engine, and hit the seat.

"Punch it," I said, and Nikki hit the switch. We were ten feet off the surface of the bay and falling. I heard the hiss of the propane, the *whump* of the burner.

And then it was quiet. Too quiet.

"It's awfully quiet?" Nikki said. I could smell the ethyl mercaptan. I looked at her and then down at the water. Things were moving down there in the cold depths.

Nikki reached up with something yellow in her hand. A lighter. She flicked it, and a big blue and orange ball erupted up into the envelope.

"I thought pilots were always prepared," she said.

"You're thinking of Cub Scouts," I told her. I wondered if I had any hair left.

Nikki pulled. The burner fired long and loud. Still we dropped lower. I stretched out my foot and touched the water. It was cold. The airship dipped, and then we were resting on the top of the gently undulating surface.

A gull flapped in and landed on the railing in front of us, looking for food. Nikki turned to me with an ironic expression. "So, once, when I was five?" she said. "I found a bird. A sparrow, I think. It had flown into our big picture window and it just lay there, with its eyes closed. It was plain and brown, but I thought it was beautiful, you know? I picked it up. I held it up to my face. I could feel its tiny heart beating. Its wings were twitching. It was gasping for breath?"

"I think I know the feeling."

"I was five, right? I leaned over and whispered to it."

"What'd you say?"

"*Don't be a pussy, baby.* It's what my mom would've said."

"I bet that was pretty effective."

"It died while I was holding it."

"You're telling me this for a reason, I take it."

"Some birds make it. Some don't." She handed me the control. "Don't be a pussy, Gordon."

"Yes ma'am," I said. I pulled. The burner roared, wide open. The water reflected the giant yellow and black stripes from the envelope and in the shadow directly below us I could see a seal looking up at me curiously with big black-lab eyes. We studied each other for a minute. "Good dog," I told it. "Go lie down."

And then the burner cut out again, and we were truly sunk.

« »

Who knew why Google wanted blimps? I guessed something to do with free Internet access, drone navigation stations, or maybe detailed GPS mapping: hang a heavy, high-res camera off the frame, pilot it by remote, swoop in low over, well, anything. But it could be much more: I imagined Googlers sneaking into Iran by night via Google Jet, launching Google Blimps for nuclear monitoring. I saw Google's Homeland

Security division hovering over Times Square with volunteer Google Snipers scanning the crowds and always ready. I imagined them as hubs for Google Self-Driving Cars, hanging over traffic on 101 and transmitting real-time routing instructions. I saw them launching from floating Google micro-archipelagos out in the Pacific to trace the swirls and spirals of plastic in those giant trash eddies for future recycling.

The specs, which were crap, said it had to be collapsible, transportable by plane or truck. It had to hold the weight of at least four people. Other than that, we were on our own. My father had known Rory since forever, and Rory knew Larry, who knew Hassan and Patak at Google Labs.

"Blimps!" they said to Rory. I imagined their voices speaking at the exact same time, like hive-creatures who shared a Google Brain.

"Blimps!" Rory told me, a former flight instructor and his ex-bandmate's kid.

"Blimps!" I said. "Love 'em!" Google gets what they want.

"And Nikki's the CEO!" Rory said.

Great! I thought. I was sincere. I'd been in bands with passionate, dedicated people half my age and with twice as much talent. I'd worked with some incredible kids on the organic farms where I'd gone for a few years to recover after my divorce. They were younger and smarter than me, ironic and edgy. I'd taught young women to fly who had the focus of eagles and the constitutions of rhinos and who could drink me under the table. (Married one too, for a while.) Nikki, Rory said, was his newest protégée. A dropout from Stanford and a musician too, with a genius-level IQ and multiple patents already. They'd met at an angel funding event: he was the angel, she was pitching something to do with leveraging improved algorithmic processing for gene therapies. Rory had invested heavily without, I suspected, a lot of due diligence, and so now they were on to airships.

She was so young that I thought I was meeting his granddaughter. That hadn't gone well. And then I realized how much her pale blue eyes reminded me of my ex. That hadn't put us on a very good trajectory either.

"Well, what do you want to do?" said Rory, looking at Nikki. Nikki looked at me. We stood together in the old barn, up at Rory's place. My guys had spread the soaked and torn blimp out across the floor to dry. It lay there like a deflated whale.

"We're close," I said. I could feel the water dripping off my shorts. "Patch it up, order in new parts. Test down in the valley next? New electronics, new valves, patches—I'm guessing three, four weeks."

"Four weeks," Rory sighed. His hair drooped.

"You can do it in two," Nikki said, staring at me meaningfully. "He can do it in two," she said to Rory.

"Make it so," Rory sighed again, looking at Nikki.

Nikki looked at me and cleared her throat. "Make it so!" she said. "Don't be a . . ."

"I got it," I said. "I got it." I doubted that she'd caught the *Star Trek* reference. Her red hair was up in a towel. She had changed into sweatpants and a Floaters, LLC T-shirt and put on too much eye makeup. She had painfully beautiful shoulders, I thought. She held an unsmoked cigarette burning in her hand, and for a long minute we all watched it. The fire crawled down from the end and then a long gray tip of ash fell off and hovered for a moment in the air between us, spinning on some tiny updraft. Then another gust off the ocean slapped it and tiny pieces scattered all across the wet floor.

We followed Rory out into the driveway, talking logistics. Nikki got a call, looked at it curiously, and went off to her car to take it. Rory drove off in his typical funk. I could see the fog had started marching in across the bay like a cloud beast, devouring the world. The boats had lights on already; they knew they were next. Suddenly I was freezing. I found dry clothes I kept in the Jeep for after surfing.

The window of Nikki's Mini was down. When I passed the window, she handed me her phone. "Here," she said. "He keeps calling me Helena. He's calling from your phone?"

It was a guy saying something in Spanish. "*Hola*," I said. "Dad?"

"Gordie? I was just having the best conversation with your wife," he said. "It's been too long! Tried all your recent calls until I got her."

"That's my boss, Dad."

"I'm glad you've learned your place. It's the heart of a good relationship. Don't do what I did—you see where that gets you."

"You stole my phone again, didn't you?" I thought I'd lost it in the water when the blimp went down. "And happy birthday."

Today was a big one, his seventy-fifth. I was bracing for the worst.

"I keep hoping you'll move away from such a proprietary OS. I have to jailbreak it to do anything interesting. You always did like the pretty things, Gordie, even as a boy. Pretty machines, pretty Helena, pretty cars. Pretty, pretty, pretty."

It was a bad day. I could hear it in his manic tone, the lighter and more fuck-you-asshole ironic thing. His Spanish was slurred. I looked at Nikki and shook my head. It had been a bad week, part of a bad month, part of an awful year that probably wasn't going to get better and what was worse was that we all knew it. "Is something wrong? Is Encarnita still there?"

"I just wanted to speak with some *family*. I tried calling you, but then *I* answered your phone, and that didn't really help much. Though the level of conversation was quite exceptional, I must say. Then I got creative."

"Helena's long gone, Dad. You know that."

"You don't need to take that tone. You know, Gordie, I'd really prefer just straight peanuts instead of this healthy nut mix you people keep getting me. *Puta madre*, these almonds are foul."

"Nice mouth," I said. "Tell Encarnita we're still on for later."

"What's 'later'?"

"Just tell Encarnita I said that."

"*Él dice que todavía estamos en para más tarde*," he said. "She looks downright thankful, Gordie. Are you sleeping with my nurse? *Ella tiene un culaso.* You know she's your mother's third cousin. What would Helena say if we tell her?"

I hung up and handed the phone back to Nikki. "Sorry about that. He's . . . well."

She shook her head. "No problemo. I kinda knew."

I could hear the guys working in the barn, the *whump* and hiss of a welding torch lighting up, someone banging out a bent strut.

"What's 'later'?" she said, looking at the barn. "I probably shouldn't ask." Behind her, I could see that her car was filled with the debris of the rest of her life: empty Starbucks cups, a stained Stanford sweatshirt, a pair of heels, a familiar lace bra, a dismantled circuit board. A beat-up acoustic guitar case took up the whole back seat.

"He's got some land that he can't get out to on his own. It's his birthday, so I was going to take him up in the Jeep. It calms him down, sometimes."

"You know, I'd love to meet him." She smiled and the tiny ruby in the side of her nose caught the light and made me blink. "Seriously—after my brother died, his songs saved my life in high school."

"Everybody says that."

"Everybody?"

"Everyone your age." Though they hadn't toured in decades, inclusion of a song in a sleeper-hit indie film had pushed Old Dog Dreaming from ancient to trendy again about ten years ago. Kids remixed and lip-synced the songs on YouTube. Original vinyl records went for almost four figures on eBay.

She gave me the finger. "And, well."

"And?"

A pack of noisy jays flew by, squawking loudly. "We could, you know . . ."

"Can you hike a trail?" I said. "Haul a moose? Are you good with acetylene?"

"I'm trainable." Then she blinked. "Really? Moose?"

"You know he's not himself anymore. It's worse than you've read."

"If it's a big deal? This isn't, you know, like a boss thing."

"No, no," I said. "Actually, he'll probably really like you."

"I'm sorry, by the way," she said. "That I'm so hard on you."

"I know you're just trying to maximize all possible returns on shareholder investments," I said.

"You read that from a book, didn't you." She gave me the finger again, grinned and then took a shining green lollipop from her glove compartment, unwrapped it, and stuck it in her mouth. She must be all of twenty-three, I thought. Soon she would rule the world.

I went to the other side of the Jeep to change. A helicopter passed over, a shiny black one with an open door on the side. Someone leaned out and studied the ground with binoculars. Probably spotting for marijuana operations—those were all over the hills. We'd even had trouble out near my father's ranch.

I waved. He didn't. I changed in the barn instead.

« »

The paramedics were at my father's house when we drove up. I had an immediate sinking feeling. Encarnita sat out on the steps holding a bottle of mezcal in one hand and an icepack to the side of her face with the other.

Encarnita read my expression as I climbed out of the Jeep. "It wasn't his fault, exactly," she said.

"Are you all right?" I said.

She looked up at me, and I could see the bruise spreading underneath the ice. "This," she said, holding up the bottle. "This is for you. At least it will be in a minute." She twisted the top off, took a long pull, and made a face. She put the top back on. "Now. This is for you."

"Jesus, I'm sorry. Whatever he did," I said. "What did he do?"

She shook her head. "I just got in between a book and a wall."

"Please, please, please don't quit," I said, but she looked away.

I looked at the paramedic. He was an older guy with a nose like a beak, and he looked exhausted. He was startlingly tall and sweating profusely, and he carried a small, empty animal crate. He gestured inside. We went in. The large bookcase of songbooks and sheet music had fallen across the couch, and papers were scattered on the floor. A lamp had been knocked over, and an acoustic guitar—the one the whole band had signed for him—looked like it had been thrown against a wall. It lay shattered there beneath a large dent in the Sheetrock. We went through to the study, where the other paramedic was sitting with my father, cross-legged on the floor in a disaster of books and spilled houseplants.

"Wow," Nikki said. I sighed. There was a big black rabbit in my father's lap, and he was petting it slowly.

"Dad," I said. "What the fuck." He looked haggard there in his gaping bathrobe, with his oily hair plastered up one side of his head and wild canyons of anxiety carved into his face and neck.

"It's her rabbit," my father said, pointing to the sitting paramedic.

"It's a new program," the paramedic said. She'd been to the house so much in the last few months that I knew her name was Isabella, that she had three children, a useless husband, and that she loved hip-hop and appletinis. "It helps calm them down."

Them, I thought. He's a category now. "It's not exactly about the goddamn rabbit, now, is it?" I said to my father.

"You had a rough day, didn't you, Mr. Hogart?"

My father looked down at the rabbit. "You can call me Cris," he said to Isabella, almost shyly. "If you want to."

Nikki said, "Maybe I should come back?"

I sighed. "I did warn you." But I held out my hand to ask her to stay.

Some days were good—I'd get back to the house to find him sitting in front of his keyboard, drinking tea and composing. He hadn't actually played an instrument for a decade—he said the meds messed him up too much, and I suspected it ran deeper than that. But he still wrote some. Other days, he'd be moaning and spinning in his bed, spilling an unending stream of nonsense out of his mouth. And then there were days like today.

"I didn't know you had a daughter," Isabella said, holding her hand out to Nikki.

"OMG!" Nikki said, frowning. "He doesn't."

"She's my boss. A start-up."

Isabella frowned, and took her hand back. "Hey," she said. "Sorry. The, uh, nose thing threw me off there."

My father looked up. "Helena?" he said.

"Dad, Isabella—this is Nikki."

"*Mierda!* Gordie, she's the spitting image."

"Mr. Hogart," Nikki said. "It's great to meet you. I was telling Gordon earlier how much your music meant to me."

"I was rather transformational, wasn't I? Some say I still am in certain ways." He waggled his bushy eyebrows and patted the floor next to him.

"Are they both OK?" I asked Isabella, meaning my father and Encarnita.

She nodded. "He will be. Just keep him calm, and don't let him throw things. I gave him some Ativan and made him take his meds. Gordon, it really is time, you know." Isabella had perfected that tone of condescending sternness used by nurses, dental hygienists, and kindergarten teachers. "You really need to get him into an environment that can give him more care and supervision."

"Dad, are you listening? Isabella said it's time for you to go into a home."

"I have a home," my father said, glaring at me. "This one has just one fucked-up person in it."

"She says you need more attending."

"I've certainly got *something* that needs attending to. You know how long it's been, Gordie?"

"I'm not sure you're helping, Gordon," Isabella said. "In fact, I'm kinda sure you're not."

Encarnita came in, holding the icepack. The pale, sweating paramedic drifted in behind her like a tall shadow with a clipboard in his hands. "Gordon, I got to go," she said.

"You're OK?"

"The ice will keep that swelling down," Isabella said. She took the clipboard from the older paramedic and looked at it.

"Which," Encarnita said, "is why I'm still holding it to the side of my face, OK? I'll need my keys," she said, looking at my father.

"What?" he said.

"Those tiny magic metal things I use to start up my car, *compadre*."

"Dad," I said.

My father reached into the pocket of his dirty robe and pulled them out. "Well, since you asked so fucking nicely."

Isabella sighed and flipped some papers on the clipboard. I grabbed the keys from my father and handed them to Encarnita. I held out the bottle of mezcal to her, too, but she shook her head. "Got to go, Gordon. You know that's hipster stuff, right? It's distilled with a raw chicken?"

"Sounds just perfect," I said.

"I'd have some of that," Nikki said. She pushed some books out of the way and sat on the floor next to my father. I took a drink first myself and then handed her the bottle.

"Can I change your mind?" I said to Encarnita. "He's about to say that he's very sorry, and that nothing like this will ever happen again."

My father looked at Encarnita. "Fuck you," he said, enunciating carefully. "Fuckety fuckety fuck."

"Mr. Hogart!" Isabella said sternly.

"Well, Gordon, it's been fun and all," Encarnita said. She reached out, took my hand from where it hung at my side, and shook it. "See you."

"Excuse me?" said the sweaty paramedic.

We all turned to look at him where he loomed there in the doorway. He seemed to sway there, in the middle of all of us, a haggard ghost from our past. "I think..." he said. His voice was child-like, as though he'd been breathing helium. "I think I—"

Then he deflated forward onto the floor.

"Holy crap," said Nikki. "Is he OK?"

Encarnita and I turned him over. Isabella grabbed her kit and shone a light into his eyes.

"Come on, buddy," I said. "Stay with us." I imagined it was the kind of thing you were supposed to say. His face was ashy gray, but it looked like he was still breathing. He moaned and his eyes rolled around in their sockets, unseeing. His beak waved east to west. I thought I should smack his cheek a few times, but held off. "What's his name?"

"Part-timer," said Isabella. "Floater? I never name the older ones the first few days, until I know they're going to tough it out."

"That's harsh," said Nikki. "Maybe I should try that." She looked at me. I rolled my eyes.

"Barry? Billy?" Isabella looked a little sheepish.

"His pulse is weak," said Encarnita.

"*Amigo*," my father said. "I know just how you feel."

"Probably just dehydrated," Isabella said. "Come on, Brad. Snap out of it." She went ahead and smacked him, and he started to come around.

My father looked at us. "Does he need his little fuzzy bunny back?" He held the rabbit up by the scruff of the neck.

Encarnita sighed, got up, went to the sink, and came back with a glass of water. She drank some of it. Then she poured the rest over my father's head. "Happy fucking birthday *amigo*," she said. "I've been wanting to do that for weeks."

"Honestly?" my father blinked. "I found that quite refreshing." He brushed some of the splattered droplets off the rabbit and placed it on the paramedic's chest. It tucked its ears back and settled down there, chewing on something. The man reached up and slowly wrapped his arms around it.

"My name is Kevin," he groaned. "Kevin!"

"Of course it is, sweetie," said Isabella, patting his cheek absently. She made a note on her clipboard. "Of course it is."

« »

Later, when everyone had cleared out, I got my father dressed and into the Jeep, and I loaded up everything else: his walker, the acetylene and helium tanks, the fuses and the rifle. I brought his fiddle, which had escaped his storm. Encarnita had packed some birthday tamales. Nikki made room for herself in the back seat somehow, and talked with my dad the whole way up. He preened and boasted, cursed in Spanish, thumped his fist on the dash, and told raunchy old stories about other famous musicians and that story about seeing Bigfoot I was sure he'd made up.

I loved the ranch as a kid, as much as my mother had hated it. I loved the smell of the old Quonset hangar, the way the old cabin creaked with the wind. Once I'd slept out in the old orchard, down past the airstrip, and I woke up surrounded by a herd of boar, rooting and grunting. The Spanish called this area the Sierra Azul—the Blue Mountains—and when the sun goes down and the coastal fog rolls up and over the spiny scrub and scotch broom, the poison oak and blackberry and the live oak, you can see where that name comes from.

We unloaded the food at the cabin, then took the Jeep up the old logging road. It led out to a path, and the path led up to a high, thin ridge. I parked, helped my dad out, and handed him his walker. "You want help getting up there?"

He looked up the steep slope and sighed. "Fuck you," he said, his chin quivering, though I wasn't sure whether he was cursing at me or the hill. He tied the bag of tamales to the metal frame of his walker and proceeded to mutter his slow way up to the top.

"What happened to her? To Helena?" Nikki asked, as we watched him. "Maybe that's something else I shouldn't ask about."

I unloaded the tanks from the back of the Jeep and dug out the bag of balloons. "She's up in the city now, I think," I said. "Runs her own bar near the Tenderloin, plays sax for an old punk band." I dragged one of the tanks up the hill to where my dad sat and came back for the other.

"Do I—" she said, and paused. She looked out over the scrub. She tucked her hair behind her ears and pulled the jacket a little tighter. I imagined I could read something there in the patterns of the freckles on her face. "Do I really look like her?"

"Nothing like her," I lied. I handed her the tank nozzles and the roll of fuses.

"Because that would be, I don't know. A little weird."

"She was much older," I said. "Almost fifteen. She had liver spots and wrinkles."

"Fucker." She grinned and hit me on the shoulder, and then followed me up the path to where the view caught her. She gasped and said "Oh!" and then sat down next to my father and stared. On one side, the ridge looked out over the ocean and you could see from Monterey all the way north up the curve of Route 1 to Santa Cruz. The sun glittered out there over the swirling layers of fog like some fiery prelude to an apocalypse. On the other side, hills ran down to wooded canyons of open space out to Morgan Hill, and then the valley stretched to Mount Hamilton and the Diablo Range. Standing up here was like standing on the edge of a knife.

I hooked the nozzles up to the tanks and checked the pressure gauges.

"You going to let me shoot this time, Gordie?" my father said, around a mouthful of greasy tamale. "'Cause you know that I want to."

"You're asking me to put a gun in your hands after what you pulled today," I said.

He scowled and looked away from me. His chin quivered fiercely. "My ranch, my gun, my stump, my view, my fucking birthday."

"You will follow the rules," I said. "You will give it back when I ask for it, without any shit this time."

He squinted at me and slowly nodded. I undid the trigger lock and handed him the rifle. I put the key and the lock in my pocket. "Wait until I tell you."

"Where's the moose?" Nikki asked.

I filled a small orange balloon with helium and tied it off. Then I held it up over my head. "Moose," I said, and let it go. The wind grabbed it, and the balloon whipped away from us, staying pretty much at our level but moving out fast and getting smaller as we watched.

"All right," I said to my father. "Go ahead."

My father stood, cocked the rifle, and brought it up to his shoulder. He took a long minute to aim, letting out his breath and letting the shaking in his arms subside, and then pulled the trigger. The crack echoed around the canyons. Off in the distance, the balloon exploded soundlessly.

My father lowered the rifle and grinned. I filled up three more small balloons and let them fly. He sighted carefully, and popped each in turn.

"*A la chingada*, I still got it," he said. "You want to give it a try?" he said, looking at Nikki.

She looked at me. I nodded. "Why not?" Nikki said. She brushed her hands on the front of her pants. "What do I do?"

He handed her the gun. She tucked the stock under her armpit and bent down over the barrel to look through the sight. "Like this?"

My father leaned over. "You hold it under here, see? Up here." He moved her arms around. "And then the stock goes against your shoulder, *against*, not tucked in it. There you go," he said. He patted her on the ass and stepped back. "Let her rip, missy-missy."

She rolled her eyes, and then nodded. I filled some balloons and let them go. Nikki pulled the trigger, and the gun kicked and went high. The recoil was so strong it knocked her backward and onto the ground.

"It's got a kick to it," I said.

"You think you might have mentioned that?" She sat up and set the rifle aside and rubbed her shoulder. "OMG."

"Just 'fuck' would be quicker, wouldn't it?" my father said, looking at me.

"Kids these days," I said.

"You two are *clearly* related," said Nikki. She looked pretty pissed.

"Ell-oh-ell," I said. "No, seriously."

I offered her a hand up, but she shook me off. She got up on her own, pulled the jacket tighter around her and walked over to the far edge where the ridge ended abruptly and dropped off into a deep canyon. The wind gusted. I could hear a helicopter in the distance. Her phone must have buzzed because she took it out of her pocket, looked at it, typed something into it with her thumbs, and then put it back. I was surprised she still got a signal out this far. She spit over the edge and watched it fall. Then she shook her head and came back. "What's the fuse for, then?"

"You kinda have to see it," I said. I took out five large blue balloons, filled them from the helium tank and tied them together. Then I took out four massive black ones and filled them from the acetylene tank and tied them together and to the helium balloons. I had to keep them all low to the ground because of the wind—I didn't want static electricity setting them off.

I unspooled the fuse, tied one end to the neck of one of the black balloons, and cut it pretty long. "Still got that lighter?"

She patted her pockets. "Um . . ."

"Dad," I said. "Jesus Christ."

My father reached into his vest. "Well, look at what I found." He handed it over.

Nikki said, "Should I, like, take cover?"

"Probably," I said. "Darwin and all."

I lit the fuse and let the balloons go. The wind caught them and whipped them around and carried them out over the drop, but then seemed to lose interest. They hung there, spinning, about fifteen feet out.

"That could be a problem?" Nikki said.

We watched them spin. The smoke spiraled languidly up off the slow fuse.

"Give it a sec," I said. "Then, maybe hit the deck?"

"Don't worry," my father said. "I got it."

Before I could stop him, he stood and brought up the rifle. He aimed and pulled the trigger and I leapt for a clump of rocks. It was back and off to the right, and I pulled Nikki down with me, knowing I was going to be too slow. Those huge balloons full of acetylene were way too close. I hit pretty hard and she came down on top of me and all the air huffed out of her tiny lipsticked mouth and then I heard the shot from the rifle echoing back. Nikki's mascaraed eyes were wide.

We waited. "It's awfully quiet?" she said.

I sat up and looked out from behind the rocks.

My father lowered the gun. "Made *you* jump," he said. His chin quivered aggressively at me.

I wanted to hit him. I got up and opened my mouth, but then the balloons actually did erupt, with a blast of heat and light and a sound that I felt deep in my gut. It pushed me back onto my ass, and as I fell I saw my father going over, too, only he was much closer to the steep edge. His arms went up and wide, like someone trying to catch a football thrown too high, and he stumbled back from the walker and went backwards over the edge.

I ran over to where he'd been and looked down. His feet were sticking out of the scrub about ten feet down. I jumped and slid down to him.

"Dad?"

I heard a moan. I helped him sit up. He was covered in dirt, a pretty deep scratch across his scalp was starting to bleed, and there were cuts and scratches all up his arms. His hair and beard had gone all wild. I brushed some of the dirt away.

"Well, fuck," he said.

"Come on," I said, studying the hill. "Let's try and get you back up there."

"Gordon," he said. "Gordie." I turned back. The dirt had filled in the twisted worry lines. Blood dripped down his furrowed forehead. He coughed, and his bloodshot eyes looked back at me. Up under his thin hair I could see the curve of his skull. "You could just leave me out here, you know," he said quietly.

"For the mountain lions?" I tried to joke. "You're too full of gristle."

He shook his head. "Later. Think it through," he said. "En-carnita's gone. You tell the girl I'm just spending some time alone up here. Do you want another twenty years of this? Hell, Gordie. Man the fuck up."

"You guys OK down there?" Nikki called. I turned and gave her a thumbs-up.

"Let's get you back to the Jeep," I said. I avoided eye contact. "You'll feel better when you're cleaned up."

He sighed and said nothing. Then he mumbled words he didn't think I could hear. After a minute I got his arm around my shoulder, he put his around my waist, and we limped back up the path together.

Nikki came down part way and met us with the walker and the rifle. "I couldn't get the tanks," she said. "And did you see them?" She pointed, and three large helicopters swung up and over the ridge in a blast of sound. They were black and shiny. Under each of them hung a cable, and as they passed over us we saw that at the end of each was a young guy dressed in camo with a clean crew cut and a glittering new rifle strapped across his chest. They swung low. The downdraft from the blades kicked up dust into our eyes. But it wasn't so much dust that I couldn't see how those young men all stared at Nikki as they passed over, and how she watched them back. One of them waved, and after a second she tucked her hair back over her ear and raised a tentative hand in return.

« »

When we got my father cleaned up and back to the cabin, everyone else was there, all of the living members of Old Dog Dreaming. Old Thom had brought his gigantic acoustic bass and Marlena her mandolin. Rory had the silver banjo and Kobi his drums, which took up most of the cabin.

My father cursed us all out for the surprise—it had been, what, fifteen years since they'd all been in the same place?—and they all just smiled back at him and lied and said that he looked great, and I could see that he liked it. We ate tamales and grilled steaks and drank beer and the mezcal. When Marlena started picking out the opening of "Long Road Home," everyone put down the drinks and picked up instruments, made eye contact and came in on the chorus. I sat in on guitar in my mother's place.

As the blue fog wended its way up through the trees and as the cold moon rose up full and bright above it in all of its heartless rectitude, and as the owls called out across the canyons and found each other again for another night, we lit candles. Then we filled that old cabin with a swell of sound.

The deep rumbling of Thom's strings drove us forward. His hands jumped up and down the frets of that huge bass like leaping spiders and the cords in his neck rippled. Marlena strummed and picked across those silver strings, her fingers moving like a breeze across a field of grass.

We slid into "Uncertain Smile" and "Kilimanjaro," and Marlena sang my mother's parts, her voice rounding out the low notes in a way my mother never could. She nodded Rory into his solo and he ran with it. He leaned back, shut his eyes, and he belted out the words while the banjo jumped and knocked there against his stomach like a starving calf rooting around there for milk. Kobi beat on. Up under that pork pie hat he had a distant look, like he could see through the walls and all the way to the ocean. Something beautiful was coming, his face seemed to say. Soon the rest of us would see it.

My father sat with his eyes closed and a frown on his face, the fiddle and bow untouched in his lap. But I could see his left hand twitching, as though the fingers set themselves down on invisible strings.

Nikki watched us all, eyes wide, swaying and tapping her foot.

We broke and laughed and nodded around at each other. I looked at Marlena and then at Rory, who nodded his chin in my father's direction. His eyes were still closed, but he sat up straight and alert, and his bow was in his hand. Rory shrugged and nodded, and Marlena mouthed the words *try it* and so I opened up "Lay Me Down," one of Dad's best songs. Kobi came in at my back.

My father didn't open his eyes, but he tucked the fiddle under his chin and poised the bow. Then when we hit the rise of that second verse, where Marlena brings in the sad harmony, he was there. Quietly at first. He eased the notes out slow, but the song built that way, as though at first the fiddle is a summer memory that's just out of reach.

We came to the chorus and my dad built right along with us and then there was his solo and he had it. The bow flashed him down the runway and he ducked his head and lifted up, up, and then he threw out that fire that caught the air and it stretched up high above us and shined there like a flight plan to a better place. He nodded to himself and his hands jumped and he darted and weaved with the bow and built that wild bridge up to the solo my mother would always do, note by note. I looked at Marlena, who shook her head. She nodded over at Nikki, who blinked and sat up and shook her head, looking at me. I shrugged *ok by me* and Marlena nodded again and then Nikki swallowed yes. My father hit that high note, and with her eyes wide she came in on the solo in perfect pitch. Her voice was pure and clear, like ice water, and the members of Old Dog Dreaming all looked at her, so shining and young there in the middle of all of them. She laid down that haunting heartbreak melody of loving and dying with the rosy light of those candles shining on her face.

My father's eyes were open. He stared at Nikki. His cheeks were wet. I wondered if he saw my mother, the way she was before everything went so wrong. His lips moved to the words, too, along with Nikki, and when her solo ended he ducked his head again, his gray hair falling across his face, and he threw out that desperate fiery riff that embraced and echoed the solo, that drove it all home.

But then I felt it before I heard it. Nikki and Rory sang on, but when I looked up I saw Marlena and Thom did too.

My father's timing had gotten a half-beat off. He frowned and pushed harder, but then he went sharp and I could see that confused him. He sawed harder, and started stomping one foot to the beat until I could feel the old floor shake, and flung his head back and forth, but it did not help.

I could not catch my breath. It was like watching a tightrope walker fall.

And then the high E string snapped. My father made a sound somewhere between a moan and a shout and before we could stop him he turned and smashed that old fiddle against the wall.

Nikki trailed off, staring, her hand over her mouth. Then all of us came to a cacophonous end.

« »

It was my fault, Nikki said later, after I calmed him down and got him more Seroquel and Ativan. Everyone said it didn't matter, that he had done just great, and patted him on the back. But the sad sufferance in their voices only made his chin quiver and the dark lines on his face grow deeper in the light of the candles. We had awkward cake. Rory took me aside, put his hand on my shoulder and said something meant to be encouraging. Everyone but Nikki left early. I got my father into bed and gave him another sedative and then walked out into the orchard.

It was my fault, she said, quietly, as she came up behind me there and took my hand. She led me to some old horse blankets spread beneath the sprouting trees. *My fault*, she said, taking off first her clothes and then my own. *Mine*, she said, shivering, and then I shook my head and she whispered *shhh, don't be a pussy* into my ear and I sighed and touched her hip. Like a terrible wind she drew me down into the blankets and closed her eyes. I was an old brown bird, gasping for breath, and somewhere an owl called out and said *oohh, ohhh*.

« »

She drifted off, but I stayed awake. I watched the way the night wind shifted her hair. I watched the sky spin and the high satellites cut faint trails through it. I heard the coyotes yowl from the next canyon, a skunk digging in the trash, a jet from LA dropping flaps and decelerating like some awful flashing angel, and then I heard the shot.

I grabbed my pants and ran to the hangar. I threw open the door. My father sat in the rear cockpit of the dilapidated Travel Air. The moon shone down on him through a cracked air vent. He had the old leather cap on, the headset, and he was pale and drenched in sweat.

I climbed up. In one hand he held the barrel of the rifle. The trigger lock and key—the key I'd had in my pocket—was in his lap. He'd pulled the trigger with his toe, but had flung the barrel away at the last instant. I could see dust raining down from where he'd put a hole in the roof.

Also in his lap was my old spice jar, the one with the cloud in it that I thought I'd lost years ago. It was open. I could smell the cumin.

"Gordie," he whispered. "Gordie, is that you?"

His eyes were wide. He stared up at the air vent, up at that moon. He reached out a hand toward it.

"I'm here," I said. "I'm here."

"Gordie, I can't see you. I can't see anything!" he whispered.

"I'm right here," I said. I climbed into the cockpit with him and took away the gun. I took off his headset and the sounds of Miles Davis spilled over us. I slid him over and then lifted him trembling and shaking into my lap like a child, and I tucked his clammy head back against my chest. *Some birds don't*, I thought. I looked up into that terrible moon with him. It seemed so close. The music came to an end. The air shimmered; the craters up there seemed to rearrange themselves, like those floaters that drift on those ocular winds across the surface of our eyes, and I thought: what more are we than those?

Blink once and we all scatter.

Blink twice and we're all gone.

MY YEAR UNDER THE DOG STAR

SEVERAL WEEKS BEFORE he died, my father showed up for my wedding on time, riding a meticulously restored World War II army motorcycle with Jessica, his nurse, in the sidecar. I was surprised to see him so early—Ted is late for everything, and we hadn't expected him until the reception was well underway. His trademark red and gray beard trailed back over his shoulders like a flag, and he wore a brown leather jacket, a leather flying cap fastened tight under his chins, and a pair of goggles like an old barnstormer. He crouched low over the handlebars, folded over his strangely protruding stomach. For a quick minute I thought he was the one who was pregnant, except Jessica was even larger. She was wrapped in a blue-green Irish shawl that had belonged to my grandmother, and she wore a heavy yellow plastic helmet that Ted had probably borrowed from a construction site. She waved to me. I waved back.

Kelly hadn't arrived yet. Guests had been queuing up to find their seats under the large canopy, but they froze in their tracks like gazelles confronted by the first sight of a lion. With waves and smiles all around, my father pulled the old bike right up onto the lawn instead of parking in the dirt lot, and he started into a noisy, spluttering loop around the white tents and the carefully groomed landscaping. He weaved in and out of the redwoods, through the gardens, around the koi pond, past the musicians.

The Indian caterers were horrified. My dogs all started barking, from over beyond the gazebo where I'd penned them up. Kelly's parents looked startled in the way only the British can, as if they'd swallowed a piece of bad fish, bones and all. The guests didn't know what to think. Was this part of the event? Even the DJ, a well-preserved surfer from Boulder Creek, had a blank look on his tanned, bearded face.

The music ground to a halt, and we all stood and watched him. What else could we do? Technically it was his land. The smoke from the bike's exhaust was thick and blue-gray, and in the quiet mid-morning it entangled itself in the lower branches of the redwoods and hung there like a garland. Sod churned up by the bike tires rained down across the white canopy, the chairs, and even some of the guests' subtly-hip-yet-casually-expensive clothes.

I raised my hand to flag him down as he passed me, without much hope. He gave me a solid high-five as he passed. Then he kicked the bike into a lower gear for more traction and spun off toward the bandstand.

I sighed. Even if you're not in business, you've read about Ted Belvedere, the cutthroat venture capitalist. Ted is all energy. He likes to be at the center of things, and is always on a stage of one kind or another. He'd been the one to move from Long

Island to California in the '70s, surfing and living in the back of a VW van. He'd hung out for a time with Ken Kesey over in La Honda and gotten himself written into a novel. He'd married and tragically lost the movie starlet Gia Paverson, my long-lost mother. He had money in Google and Netflix, ate breakfast now with famous CEOs. Valley hopefuls flocked to him like moths, and he ate them one by one like a lizard would, relishing how they fluttered desperately on the end of his long tongue.

At least he'd picked a time before Kelly had arrived. Her father Leonard leaned over and whispered something to her mother. Leonard's face, I thought, wore that deeply etched frown easily, like it was slipping on an old shoe. Margaret nodded, whispered something back. She hiked up a shoulder strap of her bra and darted a quick scowl in my direction.

I shrugged. I know my father. It could have been much, much worse.

Finally, Ted slowed down and made as if to stop by one of the food tables: samosas, chapatis, pakoras, bowls of namkeen and chutney. He waved again to the starting bartender and the waiters, to assembled guests, and gave a falsely-dignified, seated bow to the mother of the bride.

It was only then that he, and the rest of us, noticed the Balrog.

The Balrog was a sweet and well-meaning dog, with issues. He was a rescued mutt from Sacramento. He was our first dog, and I had made so little progress with training that I'd long ago given up hope, which made him my favorite of all the dogs we'd gotten this past year. He was a mix of Doberman and

Great Dane and greyhound, tall and thick and awkward, with a long and deep chest, spindly yet powerful brown legs, and unclipped elephant ears that wrapped around his head like sheets when he shook them. At his shoulder, he stood as high as the wedding cake's third tier. He was wild and excitable, and he was very, very fast.

The Balrog was so worked up by the noise and smoke of the old bike that he had scaled the temporary fencing I'd put up, sprinted across the bridge over the koi pond, and gathered speed across the open field we'd cleared for dancing. He was a tongue-flailing, ear-flapping, brindled missile who had locked on to my father, and he was coming in at about thirty-five miles an hour.

I watched it all in slow motion. Ted's thick eyebrows exploded into action behind the goggles, and he throttled up the old engine. The bike backfired, spouting fumes and black smoke, and lurched forward. Jessica, who was about my age, looked startled. She glanced behind her, noticed the Balrog, and flapped her hands, her long, white fingers waving like loose pieces of yarn.

Ted pointed the bike back at the road, where an old, eggshell-blue wedding truck was just pulling up, and he raised a hand in my direction. Whether it was to wish me good luck, to flip me off, or just to make his exit was hard to tell, although I had my suspicions.

But the Balrog was just too fast. As the dog closed the last yard, he stumbled on all of the torn-up sod and went into an uncontrolled roll that ended as he hit the side of the bike's front tire hard. Ted promptly lost control and pitched himself and Jessica headlong into one of the canopy poles. The canopy came down on top of all the chairs, two of the waiters, and many of the guests, including a screeching Margaret.

There was smoke and the smell of gasoline, and shouts from underneath the tent. Leonard and I ran over and tried to help. The bike was on its side with the motor still running, and fuel was squirting out of the broken line. I found the switch and shut that off, as two of my cousins, dressed in bright matching rugby shirts from some British pub in Shanghai, climbed out from under the canopy and tried to set it all straight.

My father lay on his side not too far away from the bike, and Jessica was over near part of the landscaping, construction helmet askew and her arms around her burgeoning stomach. I went to Jessica first, and helped her sit up. There was a streak of dirt on her forehead, and she was working to catch her breath. She held my arm for a minute, then looked me in the eye and nodded that she was OK.

"Help!" Ted yelled, trying feebly to wave the Balrog off with the arm that was not pinned underneath him. "He's a killer!" The Balrog was wagging his stump of a tail. His ears were on high alert and he was making fake rushes at Ted, playing with him: stopping short with his front paws out, barking, spinning a full circle, jumping back.

"Somebody save me!"

While my father had never liked dogs, he had always liked attention.

I ran over and knelt down. "Ted," I said. "What did you do?" It looked like the arm underneath him might be broken and there was a long scratch on one side of his face that was bleeding. The hair went up on the back of my neck when I looked at his chest, which was thrashing around underneath his jacket like something out of an *Alien* movie.

"Scott," he said. He wouldn't meet my eyes. He struggled and sat up and took a deep breath, reached up inside the shirt with his good arm, and handed me a young, freaked-out bulldog, all chest and jowls, with a spotted coat of white and brown. It smelled of urine, and its belly was wet. The bulldog eyed the Balrog warily, and showed all of its teeth.

"Here. He reminded me of you." Which from Ted meant it reminded him of some idea of what he wanted me to be— which meant being more like him. I shook my head. I didn't have anything to say, really. I held the dog into my chest, up against the shiny new kurta, to calm it. It had my father's chins and the same ice-blue eyes.

I felt a hand on my shoulder, and there was Kelly. She was wearing a simple, beautiful sari and her hair flowed down her back like liquid chocolate. There was a delicate gold tiara across her smooth brow from which a simple gold coin on a chain descended to her forehead, like a star. And beneath that shiny star she wore the deeply sarcastic expression that I had come to know oh so very well.

"Well, the mango chutney? It's pretty *fucking* awesome, don't you think?" She shoved a piece of naan slathered with it into my mouth. She pushed my chin up for me to go ahead and chew, and then watched me with one her hand on her hip.

As I stood there in front of her, holding the struggling bull-dog, smelling of dog piss and gasoline and smoke, I knew that she was, as always, correct.

« »

That whole year leading up to the wedding had been bad for Kelly and me, and the disaster at the wedding had only put a bright cake topper on the peak of it. We'd met eighteen months ago in a hotel for westerners in Chennai, India, and it was that air of perpetual certainty she carried around her, despite the jet lag, that had initially drawn me in. I was running out of money, traveling through from Singapore, trying unsuccessfully to get our offshore developers to talk to each other and produce something close to what we wanted. She was a new VP, out to meet her development team. She managed a hundred people, cursed like a trucker, and had eyes that lit up like fire when she took me to bed in that damp hotel, a place where we could not drink the water, where men were waiting to carry our bags, pour our wine, check our cars for bombs, bring us fruit, and turn down the sheets.

But stateside, in one of my father's rental houses up on this wild ridge, that fire started to splutter. She drank a lot. She provided me with a lot of "in-the-moment coaching" with what she called "direct feedback." We fought about stupid things: dishes in the sink, dog crap on the floor, the water truck bill. She got into a massive argument with my father one night over the potential value of micro-lending sites in the rural parts of Asia which, in the end, was about nothing really having to do with either micro-lending or Asia and everything having to do with what would be good for me. That devolved into drunken insults, and then both of them refused to speak to each other. And then the satellite navigation company I'd been working at collapsed pretty badly, with finger-pointing and threats of lawsuits. As a result, I spent a lot of time off work, with the dogs and the Internet, brooding and staring up at the sky. That went over really well.

Finally I let my father get me a contract job as a project manager in a company that shipped computer and networking hardware. (He was on the board.) But the work ran long chaotic hours and was entirely without hope—I'd be on the phone with developers in India late into the night trying to understand why we were so far behind budget, why the bug list challenged the attachment file-size limit of the corporate email system.

When Kelly was at work, I had free time. Evenings, we took calls from either end of the long deck that overlooked the ocean, both of us stared down into our laptop screens and microwaved take-out. I took up sleeping out in a rundown camper left behind by the last tenant.

The dogs started off as Kelly's idea. I suspect she thought that by having something else around to focus on, the two of us would be better off. But I was quickly taken with the Balrog and then for a while I acquired a new mutt every few weeks. There were of seven of them, each a different amalgamation of shepherd and collie, boxer and pit, Labrador, Chihuahua and/ or ridgeback. With behavior problems and missing limbs and crooked teeth, not one of them was quite whole. But at two in the morning, worked up after arguing through business prioritization issues in English, bad German, and disastrous Tamil, there was something about their simple need of me as one of the pack that reached into some primeval place and quieted me down in a way nothing else, that no one else, could.

We developed a ritual, the dogs and I. Sleepless after my calls, I'd grab my large walking stick. We'd wander out in the dark, with no flashlight. It was all part of my father's land, and I'd grown up out here so I knew it pretty well. They'd all fan out across the dirt of the old logging road, my own little wolf pack. They'd sniff skunk and deer, the neighbor's horses, the elusive spoor of mountain lion. They'd bark at the moon.

There was one spot the dogs and I especially liked, out on the end of the ridge where some previous tenant had carved a small chair out of the trunk of an old coastal oak. Under a full moon you could see as far as Loch Lomond, and all the folded ridges of the canyons between us would be filled up with fog off the Pacific.

The stars are brilliant there. I'd sit and watch them spin and look for bright Sirius, part of Canus Major and just down from the belt of haughty Orion. Though you can't see it with the naked eye, Sirius is actually two stars. One brilliant, clearly visible from across the galaxy, and one small and dense, a tiny, frustrated white dwarf that is nearly invisible. They spin and dance, throwing fire, locked in each other's terrible grip. The dogs barked back at their echoes, convinced they were scheming coyote somewhere off in the distance.

Back at the camper, the dogs and I would all find our spots. I'd curl up in the bunk over the front cab. The Balrog would be at my feet, everyone else scattered across the rotting plywood floor, and after a few minutes of their combined warmth, their steady, humid breathing, my chest would relax and open too. I'd hear the sounds of one or another of the dogs dreaming and think: *Good girl. You get 'em.*

We weren't so different, really. My skin didn't fit right. I was made up of two many disparate pieces, none of them really my own. I had swallowed too many old bones. My dreams then, too, were a mixture of fear and frustration and desire: *IT* is out there in the dark. *IT's* really big and bad, and *IT's* on our turf. Just what am I going to do about *IT*? Or: I want something that another, bigger dog has, and I need to get it any way, anyhow. It smells incredible, a symphony of aromas like nothing else has ever smelled. I will bark and growl and snap my way to it. I will chase it down and catch it and shake it until it is mine. I'm sure none of it had anything to do with my dad.

But up on that lonely ridge, I tried to hide the wine and Kelly tried to figure out what questions to ask me about my father, so she could then articulate and then manage my problems. But she found my secret stashes and I didn't have the answers she wanted, ones that could be broken down into specifications and detailed business requirements.

When she awkwardly proposed, over a second bottle of Cab, I think she was at a loss for a better answer. When I hesitated, she looked away. "Do you need to call your father?" she said, sighing and staring out at the view.

And I realized: even when drunk, she understood me all too well.

«»

"I was thinking of Fiji, Scott," my father said.

"Fiji," I said. "The South Pacific Fiji or the bottle of water Fiji?"

Kelly and I sort of decided to postpone the ceremony. The guests will have a party, eat the tandoori, do some dancing. "It's all paid for, so why not?" Kelly said. "Why fucking waste it?" She poured herself a fifth glass of wine and didn't exactly meet my eyes, and I didn't exactly push it. I ignored the looks from her parents, and I drove my father and Jessica down to the hospital in Capitola in Kelly's car. The bulldog didn't seem to want to join the pack of mutts just yet—growling and snapping, trying to sort out rank—so I put him on an old blanket in the back.

He settled down there like a little king on his blanket-throne, and put on one of my father's all-knowing expressions.

Ted, it turned out, had broken his arm in two places. He got his arm set by a balding, chimp-like ER tech with big wire-rimmed glasses. "Maybe Vanuatu," he said. "We'll all go by boat. You know, it's really very easy to circumnavigate now. There are quite a few blogs I've been following of families who have done it. Families with kids. There's Wi-Fi up and down the coasts. You can get satellite radio broadcasts pretty much anywhere that will show you the weather to within a couple of feet."

"And Jessica?"

He nodded once, the boardroom confirmation, and smoothed down his beard with his good hand. "She's studying Fijian. Yes, that's an actual language. She's good with that sort of thing. She'll translate while she's changing the kid and giving me a catheter all at the same time, though they speak a lot of English too, you know. We'll strap a fucking car seat right into the wheelhouse. You can teach us all how to steer by the stars. Did you know there's no H, X, or Z in the Fijian alphabet?"

"I didn't know that," I said.

"Makes you wonder if they're really necessary letters, or just superfluous. Just extras hanging on to words, while the real story is going on somewhere else. Like children." He grimaced and looked at the tech, who started and looked sheepish.

"Sorry, sorry," the tech said. My father reached for another pill and dry-swallowed it.

I bit back what I actually wanted to say. I felt like a guy in a red *Star Trek* shirt, just assigned to an away mission. "You're not a Z, Ted. An H, maybe. But definitely no Z."

"That's why I like you, Scott. You almost tell an old man what he wants to hear. You're into stars; did you know that the star Sirius is at the same declination as the latitude of the island of Fiji? Seventeen degrees south. It was how the Polynesians used to navigate. Think it through, will you?"

While I knew he had a boat, a forty-two footer docked in the Santa Cruz harbor, I wasn't sure if my father even knew how to sail. "I'm getting married soon," I said. "And I have to do this thing called work."

"In the old Solomon Isles, a girl couldn't marry until she was tattooed," he said. "And in Fiji you're supposed to bring her father a whale tooth. Not worth all that effort, if you ask me." He closed his blue eyes and leaned back in the chair. He folded his chins up like the bulldog.

I had to wonder if he knew, or at least suspected something about Jessica. I thought about asking. I wanted to see his expression change. He looked tired, and Ted was never tired. I figured he probably did know.

"How about I just teach you the songs," I said.

"Songs?"

"Wasn't that how the Polynesians remembered all those stars for navigation? They sang them all to each other."

"You never could carry a tune, Scott. You got that from me."

Bite me, old man, just let me live my life, I thought to myself in tune. Sounded pretty good to me.

« »

"It was Singapore a few weeks back," Jessica told me later. "Or somewhere else in China." Her hair was plastered to her head from sweat and the straps inside the construction helmet, and she was dressed in a hospital gown now and had a fetal heart-rate monitor strapped across her stomach. The heartbeat rate on the glowing orange screen showed 137 beats per minute. "Then it was some sort of peer-to-peer mobile music thing out of Hong Kong that was really expanding in the Asian market, he said. What's peer-to-peer mean, anyway?"

"It's like a sharing of equals," I said. "One computer trades stuff with another, but nobody's really in charge."

She laughed, with only a little bit of irony. "Electric anarchy. I like it. It's pretty unlike either of you, you know."

"He sounds a little lost?" I said hopefully.

"Lost?" She shook her head. She looked tired. "Not really. He's seventy-three, Scott. Some people settle down quietly, and some people don't. Ted is a working dog who just needs a new rabbit to hunt. He's a hell of a guy for someone his age. His mind just spins faster than minds really should. Hand me that Coke, will you?"

"Should you really be drinking that?"

"No." She drained the rest of the can. "Zippy and I, though, we like our little caffeine hit." She patted her stomach. "It's how we keep up. Do you have a smoke? Just kidding. You look a little lost yourself, you know."

I shook my head. "Maybe I need the caffeine."

"Your problem isn't keeping up, Scott. Your problem is deciding just where else it is you're trying to go."

She was a little right, though not entirely. Compared to Ted, everyone appeared a little lost. We looked at each other, and then I looked away and studied the remote control for the hospital bed. You could put the back up and the feet up separately. You could fold someone in half. There was a needle taped into a vein on her left hand that ran up to a bag hanging from a silver pole. The small clear drops looked like tequila, but probably weren't.

I put my hand on the lower part of her stomach. "So, come on—seriously, this time. Boy or girl?" I imagined the kid in there, upside-down and eyes wide open, staring at me with giant anime eyes through Jessica's translucent skin.

"Definitely one of the two." Jessica smiled sadly, took my hand, and put it back in my own lap. "Won't be long now, will it, bucko? And then *boom*, all of our galaxies will tremble."

« »

Jessica never actually told me I was the father. Most people assumed it was Ted. Jessica was more than his nurse, that was clear—she accompanied him to business events, traveled with him abroad. *Nurse* was kind of a joke between them, given the age difference. But neither of them ever spoke about the details of their relationship. I had never seen them overtly physically affectionate, though I recognized from a distance a deeper connection that was more than professional. It took a lot to keep pace with my father, both physically (he was still active at the Santa Cruz rock-climbing gym) and mentally, and I didn't know if Jessica knew that I knew about Ted's vasectomy, which he'd had done when I was a teenager.

It had been one of those early-morning walks. The summer fogs had just started coming in the evenings, but they were starting slowly. The leaves were crisp and brittle from the daytime heat and Cal Fire had been on high alert for a month. A large fire that would be traced to an exploding meth lab had ravaged thousands of acres out near Felton, and fires had been burning giant redwoods down in Big Sur for some time.

Around 3 a.m. I hung up on India, and went out to get the dogs. Their paws left prints in the drifting ashes as the eight of us went up the road in a loose pack. The air smelled of smoke. We went out to the overlook again. Along the way, the dogs sniffed around a red Mini I recognized, parked along the side of the logging road, where the path broke off along the ridge.

And out at the overlook, there she was, sitting in the old stump chair. I was surprised—it was Ted's land, his newly built house was on the same road, up about a mile, but since Ted was never home I rarely saw anyone on it. The dogs were ecstatic

and they swarmed around her, begging and preening for attention, their back ends waggling.

I sat down beside her, trying to keep from doing the same
thing. She was in a glittery black dress and her hair was up,
though she had changed into running shoes for the path. She
was taking refuge, she said, from yet another business meeting.
She had one of my dad's small telescopes in her lap. The moon
was high and half full, peering in between the rushing clouds
and smoke.

The dogs calmed eventually and settled around us. We talked about Ted; he'd been entertaining some potential investors
and some start-up CEOs and CFOs. Jessica sighed, said she
didn't like the smell of desperation, the egos, the hyperbole. We
talked about her. She and I had grown up in different parts of
these same mountains. Her father was still a librarian in Santa Cruz. Her mother had grown pot and sold real estate. Their
old house was deep in the redwoods, where the sun never really
reached, and where everything was damp most of the time. They
had raised goats and chickens and grew their own mushrooms.

I talked about the stars. We used her telescope and I pointed out Rigel and Betelguese, both in the constellation Orion. I
told her about how the Egyptians would know the Nile would
flood when they saw Sirius rise just before the sun. I talked
some about my mother, who I generally never spoke of. I had a
few memories of her deep, rich voice, the feel of her hand on my
hair, that I played over and over in my head. Sometimes, I said,
I'd watch her movies. There was an action flick where she was

the naïve woman detective on the trail of a serial killer in rural Idaho. In another, she was the bright, eager young teacher who helps bring an abused autistic child out of his shell. She was on a third marriage now, living in Miami and invested in a chain of steak restaurants.

"You don't seem yourself, Scott," she said. A stray piece of ash landed on her cheek, and I brushed it away. She was right. I didn't know who I was. I was somewhere in the hot and dry air. I was filled with smoke and fire and frustration. The dog star peered down between the clouds. An owl called nearby and as I leaned over and kissed Jessica, and then slowly slipped the straps of the dress down her freckled shoulders, all I could hear was the crackle and hiss of those far-off Big Sur flames devouring tree after ancient tree.

« »

After the dogfight, Kelly moved out.

Coming back up the hill from the hospital, I was exhausted. Ted, his arm set in plaster, had decided to stay down in Capitola with Jessica. Kelly wasn't home yet from the wedding. I drank a large bottle of Indian beer, put the bulldog in the fenced yard with the other dogs, and then collapsed on my bunk in the trailer. I had dark dreams of islands and oceans, of dark stars and bright ones all in orbit around each other, of a mountain lion living under the rental house, chewing on a moving, breathing doll, and I woke suddenly to the sound of Kelly screaming.

I threw open the door of the trailer, and saw the dogs in a pile. There was dust everywhere. Kelly was at the gate to the dog pen, a bottle of wine in her hand and her sari in disarray, and one of my cousins was in the middle of the dogs. He had one of the smaller ones by the collar. Kelly's mouth was open. She was staring at one of the dogs, a shepherd, who lay motionless in the dirt just on the other side of the fence, and she either could not or would not move.

I yelled, and waded into the middle of the dogs. I had never seen it this bad. The dogs would growl at one another sometimes, over a toy or a bone, but I'd never seen a fight with all of them involved. One of them latched onto my calf and ripped my pants leg. Another yelped as I got my arm around its neck and pulled it backward. I kicked and jerked at collars, and yelled to Kelly or my cousin to get the hose. My hand was bleeding, and I wasn't sure how that had happened.

When I got to the center of the pile, I saw that the new bulldog was planted firmly over the Balrog, with his teeth locked on the Balrog's throat. The Balrog rolled his eyes and whimpered, working his mouth uselessly. For all his restlessness and incorrigibility, he wasn't a fighter. He was bleeding from some bites along the ribs, and looked pretty torn up in the pits where the forelegs met his deep barrel chest. The bulldog shook him, and shook him again.

I grabbed hold of the bulldog's collar and pulled, but the dog was too strong. I kicked it, got right down in its face and yelled and slapped it, but the dog looked through me with those intense blue eyes, so much like my father's. I took the hose from my cousin and set it on full and pointed it up the dog's nostrils.

It seemed to go on forever. The world stretched out, and there were long stretches of time between heartbeats where there was nothing but me and those two dogs. The Balrog kicked futilely with his back legs. The bulldog growled and shook him, so hard I was worried his neck was broken. Finally, I got behind the bulldog and grabbed him by the back legs, up behind the knees, while my cousin held the hose. The dog sneezed and released the Balrog's throat, and I dragged it backward, out of the fence and over to the trailer. There was blood in its mouth. I'm ashamed to say I hit it, probably more than once, and then I threw the dog into the trailer and slammed the door behind it.

We had to put three of the dogs down that night, at the emergency vet clinic in Soquel. Two others needed stitches in their pits and along their rib cages where skin had been torn loose. The staff there said they'd never seen anything like it, and for a time I was concerned they would be calling the County Animal Services on us, though it was plain they could see how distraught we were. Kelly was haggard and exhausted. My cousin was just awkward. I didn't know him well and he didn't know us, and in the way he hovered near the door, checking his iPhone, I saw he was working to figure out just what his obligation was, just how much of us he needed to put up with before he could make a socially acceptable exit. I didn't blame him.

The Balrog died that night, and I think a part of me did too. The vet was genuinely apologetic as she slid in the needle and slowly depressed the plunger. From opposite sides of the small, white room Kelly and I watched his eyes cloud over, his legs relax.

On the way out, she paid the bill, and then handed me the car keys.

"Tell him he wins," she said. "I give up."

I didn't ask who she meant. I didn't have to.

She climbed into my cousin's rental car, and they drove off together into the fog.

« »

I put the keys in my pocket and then I just walked. I believe my mind was empty of everything I had held so tightly that year. I turned left out of the emergency clinic and walked down 41st Street, past the malls and the surf shops and the sushi places. When I hit the end I walked up along the coast. It was probably close to 3 a.m. by then, and everything was wrapped in a mist so deep and salty that for a while I walked with my hands straight out in front of me. Streetlamps were tiny, distantly spaced stars. I walked along the beach, and could hear but not see the fierce roaring of the ocean, waves coming all the way from the other side of the world and breaking here, on these sands.

When I found myself at the Santa Cruz Harbor, I walked the docks at random until I found what I thought was my father's boat. It was long and lean, a sleek deep-water vessel made of shining fiberglass and steel, and it rolled quietly with the tide.

I climbed onboard, unsnapped the cover that lay across the cockpit, and went below. The boat had power in from the docks, and I turned on some lights. It was an elegant cabin, lined in carefully polished teak, the brass instruments shiny. I pulled papers from the chart table, sheets and mattresses from the bunks. I had to go back out to the docks to find some fuel with a spare fuel can, but it wasn't difficult.

I found the matches in a shallow drawer by the stove.

Back up on deck, I lay down near the bow. The fog was still dense, and it wouldn't clear for many more hours, but I imagined I could see through it, see all of those millions of stars out there, and in particular see the two stars of Sirius up close. They spun tightly around each other, straining to the very outer edges of their orbits, yet always getting pulled back in.

The boat began to kindle beneath me, and before I jumped for the dock I thought about how some day someone far away on one of those spinning stars might see my light. I would be hot and fierce, fiery and brilliant. Any day now, I would burn back at them with an inferno all my own, one that had been here when the universe was formed, one that burned with the hot breath of all the broken animals of the world.

THE NIGHT WITCHES

Months before the fire—the big one that cuts up through the homes in our hills like a plane through a flock of doves—I see Rochelle in the street. It's a Sunday. She has her hand in some guy's pocket. Her hair is paler than I remember it, and it hangs awkwardly around her face like she still cuts it herself. She is tanned, broken-in, like she's been living outdoors all these years.

"Is that Rochi?" I ask Hope, forgetting that Hope never knew Rochelle.

Hope is pointing out the pneumatic metal ostrich to Noah as it hisses and clanks past us. He studies it from up on Hope's shoulders with a look like he's swallowed a spider. It's a moment of summer in Santa Cruz as drawn by Miyazaki: creatures of many colors leap and strut and caper in the street. Pyrotechnic children and dogs with wings grin from alleyways. Cosplay cyborgs loom in doorways. Shops are filled with clockwork angels and satyrs on stilts. Demons with mechanical jaws and painted breasts laugh and hoist lattes. A Victorian house rolls by. A snail-car shoots fire from metal horns.

Rochelle extracts the guy's wallet. He has no idea—just another Santa Cruz dad in a tie-dyed T-shirt and cargo shorts and sandals. As Rochelle tucks his wallet into the front pocket of her jean jacket, he watches a passing steampunk submarine.

She glances around to see if anyone has noticed, and she sees me watching. I can't tell if she recognizes me. Then she turns and pushes her way back into the crowd.

I lean forward and tell Hope I'll be back. She can't hear me but shakes her head in her way that says *what the hell?*—mouth tight, eyes looking back at me over Noah's thigh, and then away. We aren't doing well this summer.

I move through the crowd, peering over heads. I look into the shops. There's a store with acceptably edgy beach clothes for people who don't spend much time at the beach, a busy independent bookstore, a shop dedicated entirely to socks, a restaurant devoted to chocolate. I look down the side streets, too, but Rochelle has vanished.

On the way home, Hope asks Noah, "Where was mommy, anyway?" and Noah looks over at me from his car seat.

"I thought I saw someone," I say, looking back at him in the mirror. "Someone I used to know." Noah looks back over to Hope.

"I thought the parade was family time, Beth," she sighs, looking out the window. There's a homeless guy out there with a sign that says I NEED BEER.

Noah looks back at me. I shrug in the rearview mirror and smile at him, but then he looks out the window, too. On his side, we're passing an ice cream place that has flavors like honey-fig-ricotta and lemon basil.

"Who's up for ricotta ice cream?" I ask.

But Hope just leans over and turns on the kid music, louder than any of us really likes it.

«»

I wonder if I imagined her. I look for her on Facebook. No luck. Google turns up nothing. Maybe a month later, another Sunday, I'm down in Santa Cruz again. Things are getting pretty intense, and Hope has taken Noah down to her dad's for the weekend. Since I'm home by myself, and the pager is quiet, I dig out the old wetsuit. It says "The Night Witches" across the front, after some of the first Soviet women combat pilots in World War II—they flew these crazy old planes, and would cut off their engines when they got close to their targets and just glide in through the darkness. The wetsuit still has sponsor labels down the sleeves—most for surfing-related companies that aren't around anymore.

I get one of the two wooden longboards off the wall in the garage. It's covered with dust, but I wipe it down. It needs new varnish.

I bring it down to Pleasure Point, at the end of 41st Street. It's not a rough spot—mostly kids and older people, with calm and regular waves. The vibe is pretty relaxed. People meditate or do yoga on the rocks, but there's not a big scene.

I'm messing around in the water for an hour before my thoughts turn off and my body can remember what it is there to do, and then I finally get some good rides in. My head moves into that place where time and words evaporate. I'm part of the rising swell of the wave, the curve of gusting wind, the spill and spread of the water up onto the shore. When at last I climb out and sit on the rocks, I actually enjoy eating soup out of a thermos.

"Beth?" a woman's voice says. "I didn't think it was you, but then I saw the suit." She is smoking a cigarette in the middle of the yoga moms, wearing the same jean jacket. Her face is startlingly thin and the hand that holds the cigarette looks like a claw, but she has that same old nervous smirk on one side of her face. She has her hair pulled back in a dirty rubber band.

"Rochi?" I say. I look at the yoga moms to see if they see her, too. Confirmed: frowns, grimaces—someone waves smoke away from her face and makes exaggerated coughing noises. Rochi always could make an entrance. She stands up, tosses the cigarette into a tide pool, and comes over. We both start to say something at the same time. We stop, do it again, and then I laugh, nervously, and she smirks.

"Sorry," I say. "I'm a little out of practice at this."

"At talking to ghosts? Old Bethie," she says. "Just hug me. I can't steal your wallet when you're wearing a wetsuit. Particularly that one."

So I hug her, gingerly, though I'm mostly dry by then.

"I won't break, you know," she says, and pulls me in tighter.

"That *was* you," I say, after a minute. "At the parade. Jesus, Rochi."

She shrugs, jerkily. "It comes back easier than you think," she says. "Like watching *X-Files* or eating tofu. You look like you're doing all right. A little beat up, maybe, but all right."

"Little house up in Felton," I say. "Driving the hill."

"Wild Beth Tompkins, working in Silicon Valley?"

"Kid's got to eat," I say, without thinking.

She looks away, at the water. Her foot is tapping out a beat. Somewhere a yoga mom starts chanting.

"I noticed the ring," she says, after a moment.

"I'm sorry," I say. "That was tactless."

"That you have a kid?"

"Just . . ." I shake my head.

"It's been ten years, Beth. I bet you're still a good parent."

"Actually, I suck." I know it. Noah knows it. Hope seems to enjoy pointing it out. She got her sharp tongue from her dad—it was funny before we got married. Now, not so much. "Noah's almost two now," I tell her. Then I tell her a little bit about Hope.

She nods and looks away. Then she says, "Well, I'm glad to hear you have a kid, anyway. Anything left in that thermos?"

I shake my head. "Come on," I say. "I'll buy you some fish."

I throw on some clothes from the van, clip the pager to my belt, and we walk to the Pink Godzilla, a sushi place up the street. I order a couple of rolls.

"Do you remember that move?" she says, after the waiter drops off the saki. "The one that always worked on guys?"

"The Tuck and Nip?" I laugh. After high school, Rochi and I had lived with a bunch of other teens and twenty-somethings at a rundown place over in east Santa Cruz. A guy we called Trustafarian Bob owned an old Victorian with a bunch of land, and someone had parked an old school bus there. A bunch of us would ride the bus downtown on the weekends to see what we could acquire: watches, jewelry, handbags, wallets. Rochi and I would team up. We'd pick an older guy, maybe in his forties. One of us would pass by, drop something, and bend over to get it, making sure our shirt was really loose in front. The other one would pick the guy's pocket.

"I doubt that'd work too well now," I say.

"You might be surprised," she says, with that smirk again. "You just have to keep adjusting your targets."

We had used that move out on the water, too—one of us would flash the competition, the other would grab the great wave. We brought back trophies and, frankly, the competition had never complained.

The fish comes. The pager goes off, but it's not for our station so I switch it over to the quiet setting. Rochi breaks apart the chopsticks and rubs them against each other to smooth them out, and I notice how knobby her wrists look. Then she purses her lips as she examines each roll, deciding, and the slanting sun coming in through the bank of windows lights up her face. I can see the spider-lines that fill up the hollows under her eyes, the deep grooves in her neck down into the hollow of her collar, where her clavicle pushes out against the dirty skin. I want to put my hand against it, to push it gently back in.

"You a cop now or something?"

"Fire department in Felton," I say, around a tuna roll. "I volunteer—just got in last year."

"So you're not going to arrest me."

"Don't sound so hopeful," I say. "It's still early."

She is passing through with friends, she tells me. They met at Burning Man where she'd put on a big art piece like she used to do back at T-Bob's, this one an elaborate modern dance choreography of enemy "mimes" and "robots." The mimes just wanted to do their miming. The robots wanted to control everything, and everyone was naked—I gathered it was basically an anti-capitalist manifesto made arty and more confusing. Burning Man was a lot like our old days in Santa Cruz, I gather. Just less water.

T-Bob's house was always the center of an event, and people drifted in and out every few days around the small core group of us. Rochi and I watched them come and go from our bay window on the second floor. Some nights there'd be more than a hundred people there—students from the high schools and UCSC, surfers passing through and living in their Microbuses, anarchists and trustafarians (sometimes with kids in tow), people off the street who didn't seem too crazy or smell too bad. Phish even played there once. Mornings we'd be up and out early, to catch the tide, and we'd have to pick our way across half-dressed piles of sleeping people just to get out the door.

"So some of the mimes and robots are living in a negotiated peace at someone's camp out past Bonny Doon," Rochelle says. And after a string of bad relationships, she adds, she isn't seeing anyone in particular right now.

She is brittle around the edges, her movements speeded up and a little too precise, like a bird's. She looks at me, at the door, at my lips, at the sushi, at my chest, at the guy sitting next to us, and then back at me in the course of a few seconds. She doesn't eat much.

"So," she says. "Hope?"

I tell her the facts: we were tech writers together at Cisco, with the exciting challenge of documenting commercial Internet router specifications. I was drawn in by the way she could command the attention of a room full of engineers with her sarcasm. She liked my surfer slang. We got married as soon as we could.

I let Rochi know that Hope and I were having a rough time. The hours that Valley companies expect. The amazing logistical overhead that one tiny human requires. "You know how it goes," I say.

"I don't," she says. She reaches across the table and takes my hand. I can feel the bones in her fingers. "But then I never thought of you as the conventional, settling down type." I get lost in those eyes for a minute. They are eyes out of the past, clear and smart and blue.

I don't say how much having a kid changed things for me. How it brought things up from before that I wasn't ready to deal with. I don't talk about how Hope carries my slack. When Noah cries now, he wants Hope. When he's happy and wants to play, usually lining up dominos in dot order, or arranging his cars by color and size, he wants Hope. When he's ready for bed, he'll only let Hope tell him stories—the same ones, the same order. I sit out on the steps, tracking wave heights on my cell phone and listening to the fire dispatches. I'm stuck somehow, and the two of them are moving on together without me.

"Have you ever gone back?" I ask. "To T-Bob's?" It's late in the afternoon. She hasn't eaten much and neither have I, but we have put away a lot of sake. We've talked a lot, so much that it almost feels like it did back then.

She shakes her head. "I'm not sure I could. You?"

I avoid that whole part of town. It's like the whole space has been encapsulated in some sort of bubble, and I don't have the right equipment to break in.

But maybe now I do.

"Hope took Noah to her dad's for the weekend," I say carefully. "Maybe we should?"

"Maybe we should what?" she says, looking at me sideways, her eyes all huge and innocent.

I blush. "Go down to T-Bobs," I say. "You and me." I can feel the ocean underneath me again, a wave rising up, rocks ahead.

"Is that a metaphor?"

"It's just a drive," I say. "Right?"

"I hear T-Bob is still there, you know?"

"He's a doctor, I heard."

"I heard he was a vet."

I pay the check, and we climb into the van. We head up along the coast, past all of those low, flat houses the surfers rent—the kind we had planned to get someday. I get lost once, it's been so long, and I have to turn around at a downtown trailer park. When we pull up, it's clear the old house hasn't been kept up. Paint is peeling on the ocean-facing side. One of the big picture windows has a hole covered over with cardboard and duct tape. The roof of the porch is pulling away from the rest of the house and taking some of the siding with it, and there are bicycle parts and the back end of an old Chevy in the lawn.

"Should we knock?" Rochi says.

"If you want to get shot."

"Seriously. Come on." She gets out of the van, and crosses the street. She opens the gate and waves me over. I follow reluctantly. There are stacks of magazines and papers rotting on the front porch next to black bags of trash.

"Rochi..."

"One knock," she says, and reaches over.

But the door flies open before she can touch it. A shirtless guy stands there in underwear and flip-flops. He's twenty-two or twenty-three. There's a tattoo of the Oakland Raiders logo on the side of his unshaven neck. "The fuck you want," he says.

He looks at Rochi first, then me, then back at her. I take a step backward, raising a hand to apologize—for what, I don't know. But he's looking at Rochi in a strange way. "I told you people you can't come here," he says. "Fuck! If you want to buy you have to talk to fucking Toby, you can't bother me at fucking home."

"We don't want anything," I say. "We used to live here. We were just driving by."

"Right," he says, looking at Rochi. "Fuck off of my porch," he says, and slams the door.

"What an asshole," I say.

Rochi frowns, bites her bottom lip. Then she looks back. "My, my. T-Bob's looking younger every day," she says and starts laughing.

I don't know why it's so funny, but I start laughing too, so much that tears start coming out of my eyes. "Nice tighty-whities, too," I say, and we both crack up again. We get back in the van. I head north. I pull over up past the surfer statue on Route 1, beyond the stretch of UCSC stuff, food co-ops, the Mongolian restaurant, the micro-breweries. The full moon is up early. We can see surfers moving across the sea like water spiders.

"Look," says Rochi, leaning across me and pointing. "Look at that."

I follow the line of her finger, and see two young women in matching wetsuits, surfing together. They're pretty good. As we watch, a huge wave rises and they both scramble for it. After a shaky moment, they're both up and shooting along the surface of the water together.

I know just what that feels like. It feels like flying through the dark sky on the back of a broom. My heart is racing, and I can smell Rochi there in the van—cigarettes, and something else.

She turns to me with a serious look on her face. Then she closes her eyes and leans in closer.

I catch my breath and lean back a little.

"Rochi," I say, after a minute. I wave my hand in the air between us. "I don't think these are the droids you're looking for."

She sighs and sits back in the seat. "I should go home and rethink my life?" she says with a smirk.

I nod, and put on a grin, too. "It's been a long—"

"Don't," she says. "I get it. Wild Beth really has settled down after all. At least a little bit."

"I'm not so convinced. But maybe you should come up to Felton," I say.

"Come up and see ya sometime?" she says. "Meet the family? There may be an alternate timestream in which that happens, Beth Tompkins. But I'm not sure it's the one we're all floating in right now."

I drive her back to her car, a beat-up old Corolla. I hug her, kiss her cheek and watch her drive off.

Only later do I realize my wallet is missing. Which you'd think would have pissed me off, but between us Witches it was actually kind of funny.

I assumed I'd never see her again.

« »

All that fall, I listen to the local fire dispatches whenever I can, and carry my pager everywhere, set to the mode that lets you hear all of the calls, all of the chatter. I haven't been in the department long, and I try to get out on as many calls as I can. It's not glamorous. I go out on smoke checks, which are mostly charcoal grills or people using woodstoves when they shouldn't be. I help handle a vehicle fire on Highway 17, and get to direct the traffic until the CHP shows up. It's not that I'm a woman—I'm not the only one, and all the guys are really great about making me feel like a part of the department. I'm just new.

I spend time surfing, too. I work my way back up from Pleasure Point to Natural Bridges, and from there start heading up to just north of Davenport and Waddell Creek, where all the windsurfers go. I'm not the only person in my thirties on the water, but I am the only one who rides a big redwood longboard. It's large enough to be what's called an SUP now, a stand-up paddleboard, and many people confuse it with one. I get a nickname, "Old School," and that kind of pleases me.

Crazily enough, as I spend more time surfing, Hope and I begin to get along better. Things aren't perfect, of course. It's a little better with Noah. But some days, Hope will actually leave him with me, and I'll take him down to see the waves. I tell him about surfing. I hop up on a guardrail to show him some of the stances, and even get a laugh sometimes.

I start sleeping better, too. And sometimes when I reach out for Hope in the early morning, she's there. I tell her about seeing Rochelle, about some of the time at T-Bob's house—things I'd never mentioned before.

I don't talk about the other kid, though. Not sure I ever will.

Rochi and I had been winning a lot of competitions when he first showed up. Dark brown eyes caked with gunk. He couldn't have been more than three. His mother was a white Rasta chick with big breasts and dreadlocks and a fake Texas accent who passed through for a month. When she headed on down to Baja she left him behind. He didn't even have a name, at least not one that any of us knew. He drifted from couple to couple before he landed with Rochelle and me. When we ate, he'd bring over his bowl of tofu and greens and climb up into a chair between us. When we went surfing, he'd ride along in the beater car and sit in the sand, staring out at us. He began sleeping in our room, on a mattress we put at the foot of our bed. Rochelle started dressing him in the morning.

He was ours to play house with, and we both fell hard for him. He was a late talker—I think we taught him his first words, the names of different surfing moves: The pig-dog. The kick-out. The floater. The tail-slide. He could strike different poses on the longboards when we called them out, sort of a party trick around the big bonfire in the yard. After a year of him being with us, Rochi got him his own tiny Night Witches wetsuit, and we started taking him out on some easy waves, close to shore. The kid was a natural.

We named him Nate, after Rochi's brother. Sometimes at night, he'd climb up into the bed between us. He snored like a little grizzly.

It didn't end well, of course. Two years later, almost to the day, the white Rasta woman came back for him, full of official remorse that we suspected had more to do with her ability to collect child support. Nate didn't even remember her, but she insisted he was going to come with her back to Austin. She got into an argument with Rochi that escalated into a fight. Nate started screaming, and the Rasta turned and smacked him. Rochi went after her with a knife and cut her, pretty badly.

When the woman got back from the emergency room, she brought a pair of cops. There wasn't much we could do. The woman left, pulling a bruised, sobbing Nate—still in his Witches wetsuit—behind her.

We never saw him again. It was the beginning of the end for the Witches, and for Rochi and me. Rochi started drinking more, and went deep into all of the pharmaceutical options available at T-Bob's.

We stopped competing—stopped surfing altogether. I quietly moved back in with my parents. I think I was gone a week before she noticed.

« »

The night of the Swanton Canyon fire, I wake to the sounds of the pager screaming. Unusual winds had been howling all that week. A meth lab out west of Bonny Doon had been raided and a camper went up in a massive fireball. It started a blaze that spread across a hundred acres in minutes. Then five hundred. Then a thousand.

I hear the first engine out of Bonny Doon dispatched, and then I hear them report back—the fear and intensity in the captain's voice when he says just how bad it is, how much it's spread already, and how fast it's moving. Every station has its own set of specific call tones, and that night I hear all of them, one after another, all the stations around Santa Cruz and Watsonville and then over in the valley, and all the way up the Peninsula. I roll over to wake up Hope, but she is already sitting up and pulling on a sweater. "Oh my God," she says. "Oh my God."

"I've got to go in," I say, as the pager plays the tones for Felton again.

"I'll get Noah," she says. "We'll go down to my dad's."

I jump out of bed, run to the van, and start pulling on my bright-yellow turnouts. From the driveway, I can already see the horizon to the west glowing an ominous orange. The smoke column is thick and black and edged with silver in the moonlight. It blocks out a whole part of the sky.

Bonny Doon isn't far from us. The terrain is rough, and the flatland trucks will have a hard time getting in to the heart of it. Cal Fire aircraft won't launch until the sun is up.

And the wind is blowing our way.

We bundle a sleepy Noah into the Subaru and throw in the emergency jump bags, though neither of us know what's in them now. At the last minute, I run back into the house and grab the laptop and the album of Noah's baby pictures and toss them into Hope's trunk. In the van, I follow them out to the highway, and watch as Hope signals left and pulls away and their taillights blend into the river of cars heading down into town. The other cars are full of things thrown in at random— flat screens and bicycles, dogs and computers. I even see a roost- er riding in someone's front seat.

By the time I turn back toward Felton, the pager is saying the fire is at fifteen hundred acres and no containment. Our station is out on Empire Grade Road, where we're working to set up a line to keep the fire from getting across. I'm late, so I go there directly in the van and check in with the site lead. He puts me on pumpkins with Jeff Powell. Pumpkins are these big orange flexible water containers. You flop them out onto the ground, fill them with the hose, and they're ready to use. We're to drop some of them up Empire Grade, so that when the en- gines from the Valley get here they'll have a water source.

I like Jeff. He talks a lot but it fills in all the air. He drives the water tender and tells me about his dogs while I drop and fill the pumpkins. We drop one, fill it up, and head back to the school in Bonny Doon where there's a water source to refill the truck.

It's an eerie night. The road is deserted, though we can hear sirens off in the distance. Smoke wends its way through the trees and drifts across the road in the tender's headlights. To the east the night is clear, and the Milky Way stretches up across the sky, but from the west ashes are blowing in. A herd of boar startle from a thicket of scotch broom and scatter across the road in front of us, grunting and huffing, and then sprint off across a Christmas tree farm on the other side. I smell burning pine and live oak but also something acrid, like plastic, which usually means a house has gone up. It won't be the last.

Then I see a person up ahead, stumbling along the side of the road.

I call to Jeff, and we pull the tender up.

It's Rochelle.

She looks like hell—all covered in dirt and soot. Part of her hair is singed, and there's a bruise across the left part of her jaw. She carries her right arm tucked in tight to her side, holding her ribs.

"Rochi! Jesus Christ," I say. She must have come through the fire, but wasn't that still a mile off? I pull the medical bag out of the back and run over to her.

"Beth?" she coughs. "Well, hell. What's a girl like you doing out in a place like this?"

Jeff jumps down and grabs a blanket out of the back, and I lead her over to the back of the tender. She's so light I could have carried her with one arm. Jeff goes back to the cab to call for an ambulance, while I hook a mask up to the oxygen tank.

"Jesus, Rochi." I hold the mask up to her. I show her how to hold it when she breathes in.

Jeff comes back from the cab and says, "There's a car with its lights on, about a quarter mile up. That yours?"

Rochi nods. "Out of gas," she says, but talking makes her start coughing again. The way she holds her arm in to her side makes me think she's broken a rib.

"I called in the medical aid," Jeff says. "The paramedics are all working the explosion site, though. We can get an ambulance out of Watsonville, but that might be an hour. Might be better if we get someone at the school to run her in?"

"I can do it," I say. "My van's back with the engines."

"We have enough pumpkins." Jeff nods. "At least for a while. Let's find out. You're going to be OK, ma'am," he says to Rochi. "Just hang in there."

We OK it with the site lead. Jeff helps me get Rochi back to the van, and then heads back to the truck. I pull away from the group and out onto the empty road, probably driving too fast. The little oxygen tank hisses, and the smell of smoke coming off of her fills up the vehicle. I crack the window, but there's so much smoke outside now it doesn't make a difference.

I look over at her, and she's watching me with those bright eyes. "What the hell happened?" I say. "Did you have to drive right through the fire?"

"Beth," she says. She puts her hand on the dash and takes another breath. She looks out of the windshield. "I *was* the fucking fire."

I'm quiet for a minute, putting it all together. "The explosion? The lab?"

She nods. "You didn't guess?"

I shake my head. "That's how you were paying for it? All of the Burning Man stuff?"

"It wasn't my setup, but yeah. One of the guys got really into it and it took on a life of its own."

"Christ, Rochi." *How'd you let it get so bad?* I want to say, but I know that's not really a question with an answer.

"Look, Beth," she says hesitantly, after taking in some more deep breaths. "I kind of need your van."

"Because it matches the wallet?"

"Don't fuck with me," she says, and her eyes flash. She starts coughing again. Then shakes her head. "Shit, I'm sorry."

"You need a hospital," I say.

"If you take me in, the cops won't be far behind."

I have to slow down, because the smoke is blowing thick across the road now. I turn on the fog lights, but it doesn't help. "Where were you going to go?"

She leans her head against the window. "Hell, I don't know. Baja, maybe. Down the coast on Route One—they probably wouldn't be watching that way."

"And then what?"

She sighs, coughs. "Look, I have to say I didn't have a full evacuation plan set up in the event of a fucking apocalypse."

I have to slow down—there's a flock of wild turkeys in the road. The sky is getting lighter in the east, and I realize I've been up all night. I hear over the pager that air support is being called in, and that there's zero percent containment of the fire. It's completely out of control.

I guess my feelings for Rochi aren't entirely contained either. I'm not giving her the van, but I do take her down to Hope's dad's house in Santa Cruz instead of the hospital. She coughs the whole way, and when I get her out of the van she staggers and I can see she's bleeding.

Hope comes out in her robe and gives me that look I'm used to, but I shake my head. "Later," I say. "She's hurt, pretty badly. Can you grab the first-aid kit out of the back?"

Hope grabs the kit and Rochi's other arm, and together we get her inside.

Hope's dad, Rory, comes downstairs. He's a start-up guy, with some pretty wild hair. "Hey there, Beth," he says. "What's that meth-head doing on my couch?"

"Dad," Hope says, "Close your kibble hole."

"Closing." Rory grins at me. "She OK?"

"She needs to get to the hospital," I say. "I'm just waiting for her to realize it."

Rory says, "I'll call 911."

"No," Rochelle, Hope, and I all say at the same time.

"What?" says Hope, when I look at her. "If you wanted the ambulance you wouldn't have brought her here, right?"

I nod. "Hope, this is Rochi."

"Hey," Rochelle says. "I'm the Ghost from Communes Past."

"Um, hey there, bleeding woman."

"I was the beta test," Rochelle tells Rory. "Too many bugs."

I pull on the latex gloves and get her to let me open up her jacket.

It's much worse than I expected. I can't tell what happened—she got hit with something from the explosion? But much of her right side looks caved in. I'm surprised there's not more blood. It's probably all internal. Frankly, I'm scared. I'm not trained for this.

I stand up and pull the gloves off. "Rochi, we're getting you to the hospital right now. This is way out of my league."

She watches me for a long minute. Then she pulls off the oxygen mask and pushes herself to her feet.

I reach out to steady her, but she brushes me off and I'm startled to see there's a black diver's knife in her hand. I don't know where that came from.

"I'm sorry, Beth—I can't do that." She waves the knife in our general direction. I can feel the blood drain out of my face. I wonder if it's the same knife from T-Bob's, the one she cut the Rasta chick with.

"Oh my God," says Hope, taking a step back.

"Fuck," whispers Rory. "Fuckety-fuck-fuck."

"You're going to stab me now?" I say. "Come on, Rochi."

"I need the van, Beth."

"That," says Hope, "is *so* not going to happen."

I hear the hiss of the oxygen from the mask on the floor, the hum of the refrigerator kicking on in the next room. A Cal Fire helicopter passes low overhead—I can tell by the sound of the engine, fast deep *whumps* like the sound of my heartbeat.

"There's a lot you don't know, Beth," she says. "I'm sorry about this. I really am. I just really need those keys."

It's now, of course, that Noah decides to slide down the stairs.

He isn't exactly walking yet, but he can climb out of his Pack 'n Play. Rory's carpeted stairs are one of his favorite things. He slides down them one at a time and comes to rest at Hope's feet. Then he pulls himself up by the hem of her robe. He stares drowsily at Rochelle, at all of us, and we stare back at him.

"Oh my God," whispers Rochi.

Noah is in his tie-dyed pajamas that are at least a size too small and his dark hair is all matted from the pillow, and I know exactly who she sees. Suddenly, it's that awful night again when Nate was pulled away from us, only recast. Different house, different faces.

But again, she's holding a knife. She lowers it a bit. "Hey, little buddy," Rochi says. "I'm a friend of your mom's. Sorry if I look a little scary right now."

I know what I need to do.

"Noah," I say. "Come here."

Noah considers me from the safety of Hope's robe, then looks up at Hope. He wobbles a little on his feet, and Hope picks him up. "Beth?" Hope says. "The hell?"

"It's OK," I say. "Rochi? It's OK, right?"

She nods without looking at me. She can't take her eyes off him.

Hope hands me Noah.

"This is Rochi," I tell him. "She's an old friend of mine. She's a surfer too. And she can do tricks like I can."

Noah considers her. Then, surprising all of us, he makes his grabby gesture at her, the one he uses when he wants to be picked up.

Nate used to do the same thing.

Hope says, "Tell me you're not going to hand our child over to the meth-head with the knife, Beth."

"It's OK," Rochelle says. "It's OK." She looks at me. The knife in her hand trembles. I take a step closer. Noah yawns, then studies Rochelle's face intently. He reaches out toward the bruise on her cheek.

"Jesus Christ," Rochelle whispers. "Jesus fucking Christ."

"I know," I say. It's a lot for me, too. "But you've got to give me the knife."

She nods. She hands it over. I give the knife to Hope.

And then I turn and hit Rochi, a pretty solid left hook to the jaw. I'm off balance from Noah's weight, but given Rochi's condition, it's more than enough to do the job.

« »

"You really should have seen that coming," I tell her later.

It's December. We're living at Hope's dad's. Rochelle is in a Santa Cruz home now—half rehab, half temporary housing back in the warehouse district north of Route 1. I visit sometimes, and bring Noah. Hope comes too, though it took a lot of initial persuading.

"Tell me about it," Rochi says. "That kid of yours is a natural, you know." She smiles at Noah, who raises a Hot Wheels car in her direction.

Rochi got off relatively easy. The lab wasn't hers, someone else confessed to running the whole thing, and while there will be a ton of lawsuits, she's only being called as a witness. Hope and I didn't mention the knife, under the condition that she makes rehab stick. So far, it seems, that's working.

We talk about things she's planning to do. Get an apartment soon in Aptos or Soquel. She's looking for a job, maybe something in retail to get her on her feet. She says she's even thinking about librarian school. I don't know how much of that to believe, to be honest, but the fact that she is at least thinking of options is progress.

And she talks about Nathan, too, something neither of us had been able to do with anyone else. "I never admitted how much that little guy meant to me," she says, loosely holding a cigarette, and staring out the dirty window of her room into the gray December fog. "How much that whole time meant. How much I missed it."

« »

Later on, I tell Hope I know what Rochi means—how things that happened so long ago can still be riding along on your board with you.

"So this is where someone else would hug you," Hope says. "And say we're never going to leave you, that you can open up and trust us and be yourself and see the kid who's actually in front of you and everything will be just great."

"But not you," I say.

"I'm going to tell you to woman the fuck up and get over it," she says, grinning. "Now pour me some wine."

I pour the wine. We're on the beach in Capitola, around the corner from where most of the tourists hang out. I've brought the longboards. They survived the fire, though most of the house did not, and at Rory's I've stripped them down and revarnished them so the grain pops.

Hope's not a surfer yet. Maybe she never will be. But we sit there together on the boards with Noah, away from her dad and all of our other dramas, and today we drink wine and tell him stories. His favorite is about the superhero Surfer Kid. That kid, we tell him, is the best surfer in the world. He rides waves that are as big as buildings, with one foot on the back of a seal and the other on the back of a dolphin. He's got smoke in his hair and sand between his toes and all around him the gulls cheer him on.

And then we put down our glasses and all three of us get up on the boards, to practice our moves. We take turns calling them out, and then together we all do them.

"*Tail-slide!*" I tell them. "*Kick-out!*"

We all move around on the boards.

"*Floater!*" says Hope.

"*Pig-dog!*" says Noah, in his little-kid voice that only we can understand.

"You think we're ready yet?" Hope asks, from down on her hands and knees. We're all hanging on to the front of our boards, as if for dear life. "I think I want to know what it feels like out there for real."

For real? It feels just like all of this, I want to tell her. It feels just like flying.

HOUSE ON BEAR MOUNTAIN

AFTER ALEC WAS buried, the issue of the lake house remained. The long, squat box of painted cinderblock with
a low, flat roof, was rumored to have been purchased by Alec's
father in 1949 for a hundred dollars. Built by an admirer of a
man named Frank Stick, who'd started his own development
back east in the Outer Banks in a place he named Southern
Shores, the "flattop" house had stood alone in the middle of a
lakeside wilderness, reached only by a long drive through pine
trees and across a stretch of rock-strewn road right on the shore.
Lake birds glided up from the long stretch of blue water and
nested underneath the front porch. Wild deer roamed through
the backyard. Alec and his brother Bill caught fish, and lost
themselves in labyrinths filled with stunted, twisted trees and
shallows where marsh grass towered over their blond heads.
They chased each other rock to rock across submerged glacial
boulders. They tried to rope fauns with old pieces of twine.

True, the house had *technically* gone to Alec, who was the
oldest, had the most artistic nature, and had used the house
for writing. But Bill and Mrs. Bill had actually used it more
frequently, at least according to Mrs. Bill. Granted, the leaks

in the roofline made it a bit damp for Bill's fragile lungs, and the décor wasn't what Mrs. Bill would have selected if she'd been given a chance—the *carpeting* in particular unsettled her stomach! And who would have *dreamed* of those lamps being anywhere outside of a thrift store? But there they were, weekend after weekend, driving up from Saratoga, working to keep the old place in shape. It was all terribly out of date and yet it was so *romantic*, such a piece of the family. The mere fact Alec hadn't left a will (and who really was surprised, Alec being the *free spirit*?) shouldn't allow the fate of such a key piece of history to be determined by some impersonal piece of outdated inheritance law. Why, Alec had hardly been married to that . . . well, to that *girl* for very long before he'd gone overseas. He'd certainly have wanted it to remain in the family.

And *besides*, Mrs. Bill whispered confidentially to her friends over lunch, after tennis—while of course she didn't want to speak poorly of the girl after all she'd been through— and it was terrible and shouldn't happen to anyone, should it? And she *was* a pretty little thing, wasn't she? Hardly even showed when she was carrying. But really, just how much of a wife could she have been for Alec, if Alec had decided to pick up and go thousands of miles away? Right into a war zone? Alone? And it certainly wasn't the first time he'd done something like that. Her Bill would never have had a reason to do anything of the kind.

But despite April's lack of real interest—it was the last thing she wanted to think about on a long list of items that were more worth avoiding—the house did belong to April, as April's lawyer confirmed. Cut and dried, no questions about it, no room for casual debate, much less argument. If she didn't want to use it, he said, it could be managed as a rental and held in trust for Claire.

April ran her fingers through her short, tight curls and sighed. The Starbucks was busy, the espresso machine droned and coughed somewhere behind her, and the air filled with the smell of caffeinated desperation. Claire slept in the umbrella stroller she was too big for now, her small right hand holding her earlobe, her left arm tucked around her blue stuffed dog.

April's lawyer was short and eager, a few years younger, and his bright red hair and pale, freckled intensity left afterimages on the inside of her eyelids. He affected a flat, Midwestern accent, but the speed of his words and redness of his face betrayed him as true Silicon Valley stock. He spun and vibrated on the tall stool, and she worried it might collapse, spilling him across the terracotta tile floor like warm milk foam.

April hadn't seen the house, but she'd heard descriptions. It sounded awful—what would Claire want with a crumbly, damp, moldy place, even if it was right on the lake? Even if it had been her father's? She had never heard of Bear Mountain Lake, or any of those distant, alpine places. Lake Tahoe, nearby, was a place where people went to ski and drive expensive boats, neither of which she had an interest in: a place between places where people actually lived, all for the purpose of recreation. A tiny house all by itself, close to where the land ended, and right where all of that snow piled up year after year—it made her entirely suspicious. She was nervous even here in San Jose. The few stretches of offices downtown felt like a light façade over land so recently used for growing prunes and apricots. As a child, April had been surrounded by a Manhattan apartment complex, one of a collection of edifices leaning over her like a pack of giant animals, blocking out the terrible sky, herded by a series of majestic doormen intent on keeping her protected.

"Don't think of it that way," the short lawyer told her. His hands left traces in the air like a pair of sparklers, and behind his excitement she realized he was thinking of how he might hit on her without seeming crass. "Tahoe has seen a huge amount of development in the past twenty years! Bear Mountain is right behind it. There are paved roads now, April. Long lines of terrific mansions all the way up into the mountains."

He sat back in his chair and spread his warm hands wide. Electricity jumped between his fingers. The structure itself was irrelevant, he said. A teardown. The land alone was worth upwards of a million today; developed it would be much, much more. It was a regular source of income. A college education. A retirement plan. It was, he said, quite simply a unique opportunity, and he was pleased to be representing her. Completely confident of the outcome.

He offered her one fiery palm. It hung over the small round table between them like a neon sign, his fingers pointed in five different directions, and April looked at it, thinking that none of them were in the direction of her heart.

« »

She didn't want to go. She didn't want to drive Alec's car. She didn't even like to drive, really—why didn't people leave that sort of thing to the professionals? But her own car was intransigent and stubborn, large and boxy and slow, like an old dog that just wanted some sleep. And despite the lawyer's assurances, she gathered from the real estate people that she would actually need to drive on the *shore itself* to get up to the house. Her car would balk. It would sink like an anchor.

But Alec's old Subaru was too much like Alec to sink. Rough and eager, maybe a little too energetic. Not entirely clean, yet with a sort of practical (if disheveled) dignity underneath the cracked mud flaps and the dented front bumper. The interior was a journalist's chaos of scribbled notes on colored post-its stuck to the dash and the visors, folded into cup holders and the nook that had held his sunglasses. The storage area in back had a tent and a sleeping bag that still smelled like him rolled up there, along with packages of ramen noodles, empty boxes of film, and a package of small, unopened Moleskine notebooks.

She cleaned it out and left his things in boxes in the dining room, which he'd used as his study. She felt again like he might be back for them. There was his guitar, his squat wooden statue of a Thai dragon, his work boots from L.L.Bean, and the unopened packages of belongings the military had sent back to them, without a note. She sat down in the middle of it all and sighed. The music on NPR paused, and outside on the street there was the sound of a car horn. Indistinct voices of passing SJSU students ebbed. A cloud slid off the sun and the front room brightened. It *was* time to get out, to go somewhere else for a while.

"We're going to the lake," April told Claire. A couple of weeks might help, she thought. Maybe longer. Claire fed herself Cheerios and played silently on the couch with her blue dog. She looked up from underneath a wild cascade of light-brown curls. "We're going to see the mountains. The mountains are like the mountains where we get the Christmas trees, only much, much bigger."

Claire regarded her with speculation, and held up her two hands vertically about a foot apart.

"Bigger, sweetie."

Claire held her arms out as far as she could reach, and looked at her.

"Even bigger than that," April said. She got up onto the couch, and drew Claire into her lap. "It's so big, you can't even see to the top of it." Though Alec had, she bet. He'd made a life of seeing over immovable obstacles.

She brushed the hair back from the stuffed dog's face. It was a colorful thing with a long nose and clumsy feet, decorated in an oriental style with a diamond pattern down the back and legs and flecks of color that looked like gemstones. It had a fluffy blue mane like a lion. Alec had brought it back for Claire on his very last visit with them, his last stop on the way to the desert that would claim him.

Claire tapped the dog's head, and looked expectantly up at April. "Oh, Claire," April sighed. "Again?" Claire nodded and tapped the dog.

And so April told her the story Alec had when he gave her the dog—it was a story about a dog family: a mama dog, a papa dog, and a little girl dog. All the dogs lived in a faraway place where they had a big house in the forest. Every day the papa dog would try to teach the little girl dog to bark. They'd bark at the bears, at the squirrels, and at the tiny little deer that lived in the forest. And when they were done barking, they sat down at their dog table and had grilled cheese and tomato soup for lunch.

« »

If Claire's toys were all in place, if she had a bag of something to feed herself and enough leg room and if the straps of the car seat were not too tight or too loose and if the *Little Mermaid* music wasn't too loud or too quiet and was started precisely when the car initially set into motion (not too soon and not too late), then April might get her to sleep on a drive.

Successful for once, April let her thoughts drift with her down the interstate, thinking about an addition to next year's Design II syllabus: a new textbook on the dining-room table waiting to be evaluated. She tried not to think of the last few months, the endless video echoes of Alec's last, terrible moments posted on that website and then on television screens around the world. It was impossible to think about, and equally impossible to think how they would ever get past that legacy. How could she? How could Claire?

She'd had the phone turned off and the cable disconnected, and she'd unplugged the computer. She'd done the necessary number of interviews and was careful to be contrite and soft-spoken and uncontroversial enough to let it all pass over. She was waiting for the grace she'd heard memory could bestow, covering things over and wrapping Alec up in a flag of goodness; she willed herself to take at face value everything good that was said about him in the media after his awful, senseless death, when in reality Alec had been just as flawed as the rest of them. Yes, he'd been a tremendous father, a concerned, influential writer, a generous and charismatic person. Yes, he'd made it his life's work to draw the world's attention to places it did not want to go. At home, April had envied the simple, easy way he and Claire interacted, and the sheer devotion she saw bloom in their daughter made her both happy and envious. Alec had been a good parent; somehow, like magic, there had been an instant bond, a secret language between the two of them.

And yet, Alec had also been a distant, absent lover and husband, a chauvinist by inclination, at times as dismissive of her as he was of foreign bureaucrats who stood between him and a story. He'd had a fierce arrogance, a boiling temper just under the surface, a dilettante's distractibility. But their frustrated, misshapen love had been love nonetheless.

As they crossed a long bridge above a wind-tousled stretch of water, Claire began to stir and fuss. She tossed her sippy cup onto the floor and whined for it sleepily.

April reached down to get it, and when she looked up she realized she was about to hit a brown SUV stopped for a traffic light.

She stepped on the Subaru's brakes but it was too late. There was a crunch of metal, the cars lurched, the SUV's brake lights flickered, and its back window flipped open.

April raised her face from her hands and turned in her seat. Claire looked back at her. Her blue eyes—Alec's blue eyes—were big and round, faintly accusatory. Her car toys were scattered over the floor, and somehow she was missing a shoe, but the purple smear across her face was from nothing worse than a blueberry cereal bar.

Up front, a fine curtain of mist was hissing from the engine and, as April watched, a dog poked a long, brindled nose carefully out through the fog to look around. One nose was followed by another as the car ran out of steam, until four long snouts were pushing and shoving for space and testing the salty air.

Nothing smelled like it was burning. She turned the music off and sat with her hands in her lap. An older man with a slightly askew turban on his head climbed out of the driver's side of the SUV and came around to the back. He reached over and put his hands on the dogs' heads, under their chins, and inspected the interior and back end of the truck, the front of the Subaru. Then he came around to her window. She rolled it down.

"I'm sorry," April said. "I was trying to hand my daughter her sippy."

"Are you all right?" He looked back at Claire. His accent was British. "Your child . . . your child is not hurt?"

"No, we're fine, I think. I'm sorry I hit you."

"I don't think you're supposed to say you hit me," he said. "Insurance?" He straightened his turban with one hand, and rested the hand on the back of his neck. "I'm not injured. Are you sure you are all right?"

"We're fine," April said. "I'm sure we're fine. I'm sorry. I'm very sorry."

From the back seat, Claire said, in a small distinct voice, "Doggies!" April, startled, looked back at her daughter, who kicked her feet excitedly in the air and pointed. "Doggies!" she said again.

It was the first word she'd spoken since Alec left, exactly her fifth word in her three and a half years of life, and it was more than April could bear. She put her head back down in her hands and burst into tears.

<< >>

"I don't know why I'm telling you all of this," April said. She was talking to Aravind over tea. Surprisingly, Alec's car was fine—some cosmetic dents to add to the car's collection, a loose hose the officer reached in and reconnected (though he said he wasn't supposed to do that sort of thing). The SUV had suffered a dented bumper and a broken window latch.

The four tall, lean dogs were tied up on long leashes to a railing in front of the restaurant, which was right across the street from the lake. "We had tests, doctors," she says. "They never found anything wrong." She didn't know why she was burdening this poor man. He was her father's age, and her father was someone April talked to a lot, before he'd died. Aravind's eyes were large and brown and he had an amused yet proper demeanor, also like her father. Perhaps it was because the tea was too hot to drink, or perhaps the accident had just unhinged the day and everything was suddenly new and uncharted, or perhaps it was because she'd probably never see this man again. Whatever it was, it set the words free.

Claire was buckled into a restaurant high chair that was too small for her. Her stuffed dog was tucked in beside her, and she alternated between drinking from her sippy and eating salt off the table with her fingers.

"Why don't you speak, little one?" Aravind held his own finger out to Claire, who extended one of her own and touched the end of it.

"Alec was working closely with her. But then . . ."

Aravind was quiet for a minute. "The dogs," he said to Claire. "You like the dogs?"

Claire looked at him, nodded, and grasped his extended finger.

"Then you must come and visit them," he said.

Claire looked at April. "We couldn't," April said, quickly.

"Tosh," said Aravind in his charming accent. "I care for four. It wouldn't be an imposition. The house is quite large—it was for the family, and the dogs and I rattle about in it like old dried seeds in a pod."

"Your family?"

"My wife, she has passed on. Our children are grown. Miss…"

"Please call me April."

"April. I don't mean to be forward, or inappropriate. I have seen you on the television. I saw…" He looked at Claire. "Well. If I can provide even a small favor to the child…"

Claire was concentrating again on the grains of salt scattered on the table.

"You want to see the doggies, don't you?" April said. Claire nodded without lifting her gaze from the table. She pressed her thumb down on one grain of salt after another, and when the pad of her index finger was coated she placed it in her mouth.

"Come with me," Aravind said. He led them outside to the dogs, who pulled at their leashes and wagged their long tails. "Watch," he said. Aravind raised a hand to shoulder height, palm open, and the dogs all sat on cue. He lowered his hand to waist level, palm parallel with the ground, and the dogs stretched out their front legs and extended their long bodies on the ground, heads still poised.

"Doggies," Claire sighed, happily. Aravind tossed each of the dogs a biscuit from his jacket pocket.

"Doggies," April agreed, reluctantly.

« »

April had never gotten along well with Mrs. Bill. Mrs. Bill was disturbingly cheerful, verbally upbeat and painfully superficial. Originally from southern Georgia, she was polished and well made-up and she had an elegant house filled with elegant furniture on the main street in Saratoga and she drove a shiny Lexus SUV. She was well connected with corporate wives in the clouded fishbowl that was old Silicon Valley's social network, and though she was only a few years older than April, she had a stepmotherly air of amused condescension toward April's artwork, her casual (all right, disheveled) appearance, her lack of social desires, her quietness.

Initially, April had tried to look at her as a cultural opportunity and worked to get beyond the superficial. But then Mrs. Bill had simply used her as a doormat.

So as she pulled up to the low, squat house, with a roof canted just enough for the snow, she shouldn't really have been surprised by the bulldozer parked out front, the surveyor's flags marking the property line. And yet she was. She sat looking at them for a long minute, until Claire began kicking the back of the seat.

She got Claire out, unlocked the house, opened some windows to air it out. It wasn't as bad as she'd expected. The bathroom was clean, the bedrooms were tidy, if a bit tattered, and the kitchen would probably have been disappointing for someone who cooked frequently, though it seemed perfectly adequate for her limited abilities. Most of the furnishings showed clear evidence of Mrs. Bill's attempts at upscaling, but there was something about the fake-wood paneling and low ceilings that lent a warm nest-like feel to the whole place.

The house had stood up for itself. It would do.

Outside again, she made a game of chasing Claire to each of Mrs. Bill's surveyor's flags, which she pulled from the ground and stacked near the front door. She made Claire some mac and cheese from a box, and helped her fashion a leash for her blue dog from a piece of surveyor's line. Claire dragged the dog across the stones as they walked out to the beach and down to the waterline. There were few other people on the beach. The sun was setting behind them. The water was relatively calm, and remarkably blue. Out toward the middle, she saw a fish jump. Beyond that, a small sailboat ghosted along, though there was hardly any wind.

As night came on, April tucked Claire into one of the small beds in the second bedroom with the fold-out railing she'd bought to keep her from rolling onto the floor. She told her the story about the barking dogs, and after Claire was asleep she took a bottle of beer out to the worn deck.

The moon nudged up over the distant ridge and shone out across the dark water. Fog from the lake rose up and shimmered. She wanted to think more about Alec, but found herself mired in a mixture of broad generalities and terribly specific details. She wasn't political and didn't want to be. War was horrible—well, no shit, what did that mean? To say it felt so shallow, so superficial, and yet to think about Alec's very public death, put up live online for all the world to see, was far *too* personal, too painful to dwell on. Even now she struggled to block out the pixelated video, the masks, the loud pronouncements that she couldn't understand, the terrible violence that followed. There had to be a middle ground, some way of putting it all into a perspective that would let her move on. The world was full of bad things done for good reasons and sometimes good things came of them and sometimes they didn't. Her own country fought with other countries that had been in conflict with each other for hundreds of years, for what she was sure seemed like good reasons to someone. People died every day. In Syria, Alec had died being Alec—crossing borders other people wouldn't, talking to those no one else would listen to, trying to bring some clarity to what that fighting really meant, to give a voice to the men and women who were giving up their lives both willingly and unwillingly for the sake of someone else's ideal. It was their voice, and it was Alec's, too. And maybe something good would come of Alec's work. Or maybe it wouldn't. Maybe his writings—carried in national magazines, published on Internet sites, many of them written in this very spot—would mean nothing. She couldn't tell. She wondered how she'd ever explain those ambiguities to Claire when she was older, when she inevitably saw what the rest of the world had seen. She wondered how she'd find a way to convey that Alec had died for something of value, when she didn't even know what that value was.

«»

The dogs were beautiful. Two of them were brindles, one was an elegant gray, the last one a solid, pure white. All of them greyhounds, former racers with long, elegant snouts, tattoos inside their ears, tremendous rib cages and tiny waists and floppy ears that gave them a friendly, comical air. They surrounded April and Claire when Aravind let them in the door—a moving cloud of waving tails, lapping tongues, and the clatter of claws across the wood floors of the huge house. "They're all friendly," he said. "No worries." Claire hung back at first, but as she stepped across the threshold the dogs surrounded her. She tossed back her tangled curls, closed her eyes, and held her arms above her head. As the dogs pressed in from all sides a smile spread across her face.

After an initial flurry of interest, the dogs trotted back to the large living room, sprawling long-limbed across cushions and couches, climbing into chairs. "They shouldn't be on the furniture," Aravind said. "But . . ." He held up his hands in the same gesture of amused hopelessness her father had used with

April. "They lived in cages their whole lives! Imagine. I thought they'd enjoy all the open space, and yet here they are. All in the same room. All on top of each other." He laughed. "It's all very American of me, I know. My wife would say I've lived here too long. She'd be right."

He showed them briefly around the house: a humongous mansion, easily seven times the size of her small place here. "We built it as an investment, of course. But also as a place for the girls to come. You see?" He pulled open a closet door, revealing women's clothing. "They still come on holidays to humor me, but it is silly to hold a house such as this to use a week or two every year." His voice echoed from the high ceilings. "My wife and I were fortunate in some ways," he said, simply. "In others . . ." He started to say something, and then stopped. "Well, enough of that. I'll be placing it for sale shortly. It will belong to someone else, and I will go back to Milpitas and enjoy my retirement."

Alec would have thought it was all too much—the large, empty rooms with elegant furniture, the expensive tile in the bathrooms, the multiple outdoor hot tubs (one for each of the three floors), the endless expanse of decking overlooking the glassy lake. Mansions lined the wooded street for half a mile in either direction.

But she enjoyed the visit, the company. Aravind served her a spicy iced tea in a tall glass and had mango juice and tiny Indian crackers for Claire. Claire surprised April by actually eating them, one after another, straight through until they were gone. He told them about each of the dogs, their names, their temperaments, their habits. The white one hoarded things: small pillows, the others' toys, Aravind's slippers. Two of them ate nothing but meat, and he cooked beef liver for them nightly. When they were walked, they could never be let off the leash— they ran as fast as small cars and had no wariness of traffic. One of the brindles slept upside-down, legs in the air, her tongue lolling out of her open mouth. He hadn't spent enough time with his own girls when they were young, Aravind said. These dogs were his children now.

They leashed the dogs and walked them along the beach, looking at the long row of mostly empty mansions tucked among the trees. And when they got back Claire lay down with the pack of them in front of the television. She fell asleep sprawled across the quiet white dog.

On the couch, with a Disney cartoon wrapping up on the flat screen, April felt the enormous weight of Alec's death descend on her all at once, as if in the few hours of distraction with Aravind it had been waiting for her, gathering strength. Her chest grew tight. She felt winded, as if she'd been running for miles. She thought she might be able to sleep for weeks on end.

She studied Aravind's face as he watched the cartoon. His beard was thick and soft and dark gray, like her father's had been. If he had been her father, there was so much she would have said to him. She would talk about how she missed Alec and how sometimes she didn't and how bad that made her feel, and about how awful his death was and how she would never be able to bear the thought of it. She would talk about how raising a girl by herself was the most frustrating, difficult thing she had ever done and yet how there were times when it seemed her whole life would have been wasted and without beauty if Claire had not become part of it. She would ask him what she wanted her to do now that everything had changed, and maybe he would tell her.

Hesitantly, knowing she was breaking all rules of decorum, she leaned over and rested her head on Aravind's shoulder. For a long minute he didn't react, didn't acknowledge her. But then he reached out, took one of her hands in his and held it.

Neither of them said anything. April felt her chest relax, her breathing deepen. On the floor, one of the dogs was running free in a dream.

« »

At home that evening, Claire ran about the small place with her blue dog in tow, teaching it to bark. She'd stop and look out a window, hold up the toy, point and then bark for the dog in tiny, high-pitched yips. That night, April told her the dog story, with an extra ending. After all of the dogs went to sleep in the big house in the forest, the girl dog heard a noise. What could it be? She opened the door and went out onto the dog porch and there was a bear! It wanted to get into the house and eat all of the grilled cheese sandwiches!

"What did that girl dog do?" April asked. Claire watched her, wide-eyed, and shook her head. "That girl dog barked! She barked as loud and long as she could. And then the mama dog and the papa dog came out and they all barked together. And they scared that bear away. That little girl dog saved all of the grilled cheese! What a great job."

"Mama," said Claire.

April's heart leaped into her throat, and she did her best not to show it. "Yes, Claire?"

"The papa dog didn't bark. He just stayed dead."

April bent her face down next to Claire's and kissed the girl's forehead. "But the mama dog and the girl dog scared that bear away all by themselves, didn't they?"

"Yes," Claire said. She leaned back and put her head on the pillow. "Yes. They were good barkers."

« »

They saw Aravind and the dogs two more times before he left for Milpitas. The first was at a small independent bookstore up in Truckee. April and Claire pulled in and the dogs were tied up on the small porch out front. Aravind came out with a book of old wooden boats under his arm. He saw them, stopped, and hesitantly met April's eyes. When she smiled, he matched it with a grin and they walked the greyhounds up and down the street, while Claire held the leash of one dog after another.

The last time was at the beach house. It was late in the afternoon, and April and Claire were planting flowers to resurrect some old dirt beds along the front of the house when Aravind's

SUV pulled up. "Doggies!" Claire cried, pointing. She grabbed April's hand and pulled her out to the road.

"I am leaving today," Aravind said, climbing down out of the truck. He let the dogs out on their leashes. "I will not see you again for some time, I expect. So I have brought gifts!"

Despite April's protests, he handed them each a beautifully wrapped package. She took off her gardening gloves, had Claire put down her small plastic shovel, and brushed the dirt off of her small hands.

Claire insisted on opening both boxes, which held intricately patterned saris. Claire's had a red pattern on a white background, trimmed with a wide golden edge. April's was red with a blue and silver border that caught the light. They were wonderfully gauzy; April had never felt gossamer silk.

"They belonged to my daughters—I do hope you enjoy them. Though I'm afraid you'll need to learn the art of wrapping them from someone who has had more experience than I."

"They're lovely," April said. "You really shouldn't have done this."

Aravind raised his hands. "My daughters are modern American women. What do they need these for?"

Claire turned the shimmering cloth over and over in her hands. She held it up to April, an inquiring look on her face. "You can try it on later," April said. But Claire shook her head, tap-danced her feet.

"I do not mind waiting," Aravind said.

So April took Claire into the house. She brushed her unruly hair into pigtails and helped her out of the shorts and tank top and wrapped the long sari around her waist, over her shoulders. It was much too large for her, and it went around and around her slight frame, but when she was done Claire went and stood in front of the long mirror in the main bedroom, smoothing her hands up and down the shimmering folds of fabric.

"You too, Mama," Claire said quietly, almost a whisper.

So April complied, quickly working the sheer material around herself. She tucked the ends of the sari in where they seemed to fit.

She stood side by side with Claire at the mirror, where the two of them were now transformed into elegant, beautiful creatures of mystery.

There were traffic noises outside, old brakes squeaking to a stop, and as she was walking to the door she heard the yelp of a dog, a shout from Aravind. She rushed outside, trying not to stumble over the sari, as other voices joined his.

A small dump truck with a confederate sticker on the back window had parked on the road behind Aravind's SUV. There were men inside, two of them with bright yellow hats, and one of the drivers had gotten out with an anxious look on his red-dening face. Behind the trucks, Mrs. Bill's Lexus SUV pulled in, sunlight glancing off the windshield. Aravind was in the yard near to the dump truck, bent over something vivid and white moving on the ground, while at the same time trying to manage the leashes of the all the dogs who anxiously wrapped and rewrapped themselves around him. The white thing on the ground yelped again, and April realized it was one of the dogs.

She ran over to Aravind. Mrs. Bill shut the door of the Lexus and stood surveying the scene with an imperious air, taking in Aravind, the dogs, and the two of them, who she clearly didn't recognize behind the saris. "What's going on here? What's all this?" she said. "You people will need to leave my house this instant!"

"It's not yours," April said, bending down over the white dog, next to the fat, soft tires of the dump truck. The dog climbed to its feet awkwardly, like a new colt, holding a back leg off the ground. Angrily, she looked up at Mrs. Bill. "You can't just take what you want, don't you realize that?"

Mrs. Bill frowned in April's direction. "April? Is that you?" She came up and took April's arm and lifted her to her feet. "Honey, just what's going on here? Who's that . . . that man?"

"A friend of ours. Look—"

But Mrs. Bill was still caught up in her own talking, waving her hands in the air. "But April, really! This is more than a little inappropriate, isn't it? All of these animals on the property! And Alec's hardly in his grave, and here's this, this foreign *man*! What if the news people saw you here, dressed like this? In their clothes like that?"

April felt her face grow hot. Claire came up beside her to look at the dog, and folded herself fearfully against April's legs, watching all of them—Mrs. Bill's sunken, intense eyes, the anxious concern on Aravind's face as he cradled the dog, felt down the dog's injured leg. "We're not exactly at war with India, Sarah."

Mrs. Bill frowned, dismissively. "Honey, what's the difference? India, Afghanistan, Syria? How many of our men do they need to take before we stand up for ourselves?"

April raised her hand and swung her palm across Mrs. Bill's carefully made-up cheek. Mrs. Bill staggered back with a look of shock and put her hand up to her face. She squinted back at April as if seeing her there for the first time.

"You little bitch," she said quietly. Her look of shock shifted into one of anger: cheeks tight, eyebrows low, face getting red. She took a step forward, and April wasn't sure if Mrs. Bill was going to leap at her, polished nails extended like claws.

The driver in the yellow hat stepped toward the two of them, his hands out in a placating way. "Ladies . . ." he said hesitantly.

"Go home, Sarah," April said. "To your own home. This one is ours."

Mrs. Bill opened and closed her mouth. "I don't think—"

But she didn't finish, because Claire stepped forward then. With her little hands on her tiny hips, her stubby, vibrating pigtails, she glared back at Mrs. Bill and threw her little chest out and she barked at her, six or seven good solid *woofs* that echoed back off the hills behind them.

Mrs. Bill's face went bright scarlet, and she looked from Claire to April and then back at Claire in disbelief. She raised up a finger and pointed—whether it was at Claire or at April, April wasn't sure.

But April didn't wait to find out. She stepped forward and hoisted Claire up in her arms. Claire looked at her and April nodded back, and then both of them began to bark at Mrs. Bill, as loud as they could.

April decided she liked the way the barks felt, coming up out of her throat from some deeper place, all guttural like that. And she liked it that she didn't give a fuck what the rest of them thought about her daughter, about her, about both of them standing together there and barking at Mrs. Bill as the sun went down and the moon started to rise, as the new fog over the lake starting to creep in on them like the gentle hand of memory ready to turn everything soft and white.

She watched as Mrs. Bill took another step back and stared at both of them in disbelief. Then the woman threw her hands up in the air and retreated to her shiny SUV, put the car into gear and sped off, leaving deep tire tracks behind her. The old dump truck followed close behind.

They caught their breath and looked at each other. "Mama," Claire whispered. "You are a good barker."

"Thanks, Claire," April said. "You're pretty good yourself, you know." She tugged on one of the girl's tiny pigtails. And while she had a sense of it then, it was really only years later, when April had found and married a nice architect, with allergies and smelly feet and a deeply affectionate nature, and after Claire had grown into a shining young woman full of desperate beauty and was about to go off around the world on adventures of her own—it was only then, standing on the edge of this same lake, with Claire in her twenties hugging her goodbye, that April knew: it had been the sounds of the two of them, barking together that had been the thing that had banished not only Mrs. Bill from their lives, but had started to chase off that awful lethargy that had lumbered along beside her since Alec's death.

She had stood in a place, this place—once Alec's and one that she and Claire still called her own—and she had opened up her heart. And here, like her dead husband, like her beautiful daughter, she had begun to find her own true voice.

JERSEY DEVILS

CLAUDE HAS NEVER made good decisions, and a premature last-night celebration on the night before his actual last night is right up there with the rest of them. Bourbon, too much of it, followed by the usual: an imagined insult, a broken glass, the slap of fists and the tight hug of the wide, bald man at the door. The asphalt of the San Jose street cups Claude's cheek like a woman's hand and carries him into a waking dream of hospital ER fluorescent lights, the smell of disinfectant, gruff nurses poking and prodding and bandaging. Then the sound of beeping monitors dopplers off, followed by an hour or two of sweaty, fevered sleep filled with country music played too fast, the four-four beat hooked to a lawnmower engine, thumping in time to his hyped-up, fight-or-flight pulse. And the ghost of his father, dead and buried Lenny Choteau doing that shuffling two-step dance of his with a grin on his pale face and a rusted shovel in his hand, his flannel shirt smelling of wet dirt and ashes. *Mon tabarnak!* Lenny curses him in French as he dances. *Mange d'la merde!* Goddamn Tabernacle! Eat shit! Lenny's teeth are the color of coffee grounds and his tongue is a blind, obscene earthworm.

The next morning at dispatch, in a twist, Rudy Roy Castigliano decides he wants to ride along with them. Rudy Roy—boy in a tux at this time in the morning, ruddy and immaculate and shining in the rising sun like a dancing bear. Rudy Roy with the giant smoldering stogie. Rudy who doesn't care about the schedule since the guy Claude works for works for a guy who works for Rudy Roy's dad.

Rudy Roy wants to ride along with Claude and the old guy named Alpo for no reason Claude can make out. To drink bad coffee? To get in touch with the little people? But Rudy Roy gets paged, makes a loud call—the tiny silver flip phone couched in a huge paw—comes back and says no such luck. "Getting a freighter in just a little while," Rudy Roy says. In the cold morning, smoke steams from his pores. "Some big things needin' immediate attention, you know what I'm saying? But no big deal. You guys know the routine, don't ya?"

Claude doesn't, but he isn't about to say so. Not this particular route, anyway. He's driven for Castigliano on and off for the past few years, but each job is different, each company is different, and here he is, the last one, the last time he'll need to look at this teenager and say, "Yes, sir, let me light that for you."

Alpo nods back at Rudy Roy and sweats in the cold Oakland fog. With a string-haired, rounded head, arms that seem just a little too long, and small, wrinkled hands clasping a shopping bag, Alpo's a graying chimp. His huge wireframe glasses reflect the etched metal bones of the Bay Bridge, the rundown docks, the guys doing crack behind the warehouse with the sign that says Bovex, the name of this new start-up venture, which Claude knows has something to do with farming. Rudy Roy gives him a locked briefcase, two hundred-dollar bills, and another flip phone. "You run into any problems, you call me, hear? Number of the cell's on speed dial."

In the cab of the trailer truck, Alpo hunches over a map, folding and refolding as they pull out, tracing roads with his fingers and whispering to himself. He looks out the window for a few minutes, points the way, then looks down at the map again.

Alpo's tiny, balding chimp head condenses all the humidity out of the cab like a cold egg. He wipes his wrinkled hand across the top of it, dries it on his pants, and then unrolls the top of the shopping bag, sorts through it, and takes out a cassette. The tape clicks into place in the amped-up sound system, and the soundtrack of the movie of Claude's miserable life begins, sung by a resurrected chorus of 1980s American girl bands. Alpo comes alive as though someone hooked him up directly to the truck's battery, tapping his hands on his knees and the dash, glasses flashing. "I know a lot of people say they're all tits and no talent," he shouts over the music. "I think they're wrong. I mean listen to those harmonies in there! Layered like cake. Listen to that timing—perfection! Perfectimundo! You don't think they had to work at that?"

Claude nods, noncommittal. The clouds break open and down comes three times the rain that's been dumping on them all morning. The truck shivers in the wind that's up out of nowhere in this paved-over country. The northbound traffic is stupid; stupid drivers, all of them changing lanes when they should just sit there. The coffee and the painkillers have moved into his hands and arms. The nerves flare up and his palms sweat so much he can't hold the wheel straight.

But then, strangely, it all passes over like the shadow of his father's hand across his troubled brow—another small reprieve. The traffic parts and they shoot easily up the middle lane. He thinks about Canada, about the view from Lenny's front porch, the one he hasn't set his boots on in years: the broad stretches of the bay between Bouctouche and Prince Edward Island on a calm day, the boats working in and out of the tiny marina, the wind filled with salt and the smell of fried seafood. With that in his mind, shining like it's just on the far side of the tollbooths, even the cheery undead superpowers of the music merge with the road rhythm into a strange sort of harmony. It vibrates his teeth a little deeper into their sockets.

« »

North of Medford, Grant's Pass, and Myrtle Creek, deep into the wilds of Oregon. The first stop is a small farm off a back road that's only recently been paved. The road lines are bright and shiny, tracked over with mud at the mouth of the dirt driveway. They pull up to the old house and a guy with sideburns—Lenny's age, if Lenny was still around—comes out chewing gum, dressed in dirty brown jeans and a T-shirt with the Hawaiian flag on it. Four hairy dogs scurry out the door behind him and run circles around the truck, barking and whining. Alpo takes a list out of the shopping bag and consults it, then rolls down his window and the guy comes over.

"Mr. Frank?" The guy blinks a few times, looking in at the bandages on Claude's face. "Mr. Frank?"

"Charles. Frank Charles." He labors over each word as if speech is a new thing and his mouth needs some time to get used to it. "You guys do that every time, y'know. I'm an old friend of Mr. Cas. We was in together. You guys should give me some more respect, okay?"

Alpo pushes his glasses up on his slippery nose. "Any problems this month, Mr. Charles?"

The guy thinks about it for a minute, hitches up his belt with both hands. His sideburns are long, and they feather out over his ears. "Never seen them shit quite that way before. Maxie, be quiet."

"No fatalities? No illnesses?"

"Two."

"Two dead?"

"That's what I said."

"The white Jerseys? Or the other ones?"

Frank Charles studies his running shoes. They're white with blue swooshes on them, and they're caked with mud. "Other."

"What did you do with the bodies?"

"Left 'em there, like you said to." He giggles once, out of the side of his mouth—a strange, pressurized sound.

"All right, we'll take care of that. Any births? Says here you had a few cows almost ready to go."

"Three a those."

"And the calves, they were all completely white?"

"Yep. I don't know how you guys did it since they was preggo before you even got started with the shots."

"How about the milk," Alpo asks. "Production stable? You tracking it like we showed you? Any changes up or down?"

"Up."

"They're producing more milk than last month?"

"Oh yeah!"

"A lot more? A little more?"

"More's what I said, isn't it? You figure the rest out. Maxie! Quit! That damn dog. She starts it. Rest of them just follow her lead."

"And you're dumping the milk, right Mr. Charles? Remember you signed those papers that said how the milk was to be disposed of?"

Frank Charles' eyes get big for a second, and then he looks around quickly—at the house, the low clouds, the silver bulldog on the hood of the truck. "I remember. I been dumping all of it, just like you said. I'm not selling any of it, no sir."

Claude shakes his head.

Alpo rolls his eyes. "How about the food intake?" he asks.

"I'm just not hungry." Frank grins at Claude. When Claude's expression doesn't change, he looks back at Alpo. "What'd you do to that guy, anyway?"

"Is the livestock eating more or less, Mr. Charles?"

"Shit. You guys have no sense of humor. I can't get the damn things to eat much of anything anymore. Not that they seem to need it."

"All right. I'll need to see your data, Frank."

Frank Charles wanders back toward the house, stops on the porch and giggles again, opens the screen door and goes inside. The dogs seem a little confused, and decide to settle down on the porch. Alpo takes Rudy Roy's Bovex briefcase, cups his hand over the lock, and dials a combination. Inside are rows of glass vials and a large syringe nestled in foam, some things wrapped in plastic, and some sort of handheld computer, flat and black and about the size of a slice of bread. All of it is surrounded by stacks of cash, mostly twenties. He pulls a pen off the computer and writes some notes on the screen. The computer beeps, and Alpo writes some more notes.

Frank Charles is taking his time. Claude pops the cassette out of the radio and turns the FM on, looking for news. Rain tomorrow, no shit. Train derailed in Texas. More bombings. The flip phone rings so he doesn't get the full gist of the newscast, but it doesn't sound very good. Alpo answers the phone, then passes it over.

"Clawed Shoo-tow," Rudy Roy Castigliano says. "My frog man! That you? Look. I know it's your last gig. I know it, my man! But look, you always been good to us, right? What say you take just a few more rides. For me. Personal. No more of this small-time crap. I mean the *real* stuff! The stuff that matters. The stuff that pays you back the *right* way, know what I'm saying?"

Claude knows. He just doesn't know what to answer. Frank Charles comes back with an old pencil tucked behind his right ear and a stack of paper, and Claude tells Rudy Roy he'll think about it and call him back. "Think hard, my man," Rudy Roy says. "You know I'm countin' on you."

Frank Charles smiles like a proud five-year-old when he hands the materials over. Alpo takes the sheets and spreads them out on the briefcase, and even Claude can see that the last group of columns was all filled in pretty fast, in pencil. Alpo circles a few numbers for show. "Thanks, Frank. You remember that today's the pickup day? We're going to need to check all of them over and get our own livestock loaded before I can pay you. I'm going to have to bring those white calves along with me, too."

Frank Charles is still smiling. It's a smile with pressure behind it in the jaws and eyes, like the whole of his face is holding something back. He nods absently, and waves them on around back to where the barn is.

The barn had been red once, but it's gray and weathered now. They can still see an old, faded ad for chewing tobacco along the one side that faces nothing but a long stretch of fields, mounded up with what must be hills of green cow shit. Flies rise up in great glittering clouds as they pull in and a dozen cows mill in and out of the structure or are lying in the shade, chewing and swatting restlessly with their tails. Most of them are the black and white blotched ones, and they're the worst looking animals Claude has ever seen—scrawny and runny-eyed, ribs showing, with big bloated udders that swing ponderously, threatening to tip them over as they walk. Only three of them are looking all right—three smaller, dirty white cows that mill in and around the others.

Alpo takes some medical gloves from the briefcase and passes a set to Claude, then rummages around under the seat and pulls out two folded packages, one of which he hands over. "Be careful of a couple of things," he says, unwrapping the other package. It's a blue jumpsuit of some kind, made out of a thin, pliable material almost like paper. "Don't come into full contact with any of them if you can help it. If you do, there's gas in the back of the truck you should wash yourself off with, whatever touches. The quicker the better and watch out for your eyes. We had goggles last time around, but I don't see any here now. They don't move all that fast, so it shouldn't be all that big a deal. Put this on, too." He hands Claude a thin mask to cover his face and nose, then shakes out the suit and pulls the legs on over his shoes.

He gets out of the truck with the briefcase. Claude puts the mask on over the bandages, pulls the gloves on, and then slides into the suit and zips it up. It's huge and billowing—he feels inflated, like some sort of circus act, half blimp, half clown. Blankets of flies spring into the air, shifting and darting like flocks of birds across the sun.

"What I need to do," Alpo says, "is isolate each of the standard animals, look it over, and extract a sample of fluid from the spinal column. Then we'll round up ours, those three whites and the calves, wherever they are, and take them with us." He points to the white cows. "Bring the gas down. I'll feel better having it close."

The cow doesn't move, though its eyes track Alpo as he gets closer. He murmurs to it in a monotone. The cow doesn't seem to react until he's right up on top of it. But then it spooks, blows steam out of its nose, and swivels its head around. It lets out a low bawl and its legs start to quiver. It edges backward into the field, keeping its eyes on Alpo.

"Circle around from behind," Alpo calls.

Claude makes a wide arc and comes in behind the cow, hands spread, enough to the side so that the cow can see him, but not far enough over that it'll have a way to get by him. They back it toward the fence. The cow shivers more, lets loose a long fart, and Claude gets a hot whiff of it even through the bandages and the clotted blood in his nose. The gas is heavy and dank and foul, a soup of everything he hates about this country. He takes a step back and his eyes water up.

"Pretty fierce, huh? I wouldn't light any matches if I were you." Alpo gets up to the head of the cow, grabs it around the neck, and sets to work. He pats the cow down, feeling along its sides and up under its stomach for any sores or strange lumps, murmuring low, meaningless words to calm the animal. He rolls back its eyelids on each side and checks in its ears. Then he cracks the briefcase again and takes out the syringe. The long needle slides smoothly between the thick vertebrae of the cow's neck. Alpo's thumb pulls back and the flask fills with a pale pink fluid. When it's full, he pops it out, places it carefully in the briefcase, and replaces it with an empty one.

They move on to the next cow, and then try for a third. It's not easy—they're a skittish bunch, prone to bolting, and the hard part is getting close enough to them to grab on. Alpo tells Claude to get Frank Charles, and they glove and mask him too. It takes Frank a few minutes to figure it all out—he puts his feet in the wrong legs and gets the mask on upside-down, and in the end Claude has to dress him. But he makes a fine sheepdog, running along the perimeter and rounding up the quicker ones. "I do this every morning," he says. "Great way to get some exercise. Maxie! C'mere, girl." The dogs leap from the porch and duck under a well-worn part of the wooden fence. Frank comes up behind the cows and claps his hands low to the ground and startles them into motion. Then he jogs along behind them, head thrown back and stepping high with his toes, pumping his arms into the air, just out of their view. He makes a lot of noise, huffing and clapping his hands and shouting. "Hey!" he says. "Ho there! Supercows, look out! I'm comin' atcha!" The cattle swivel their heads back and forth, trying to get a look at Claude and Alpo, Frank Charles and the dogs all at the same time. They shift as a group in and out of the shelter of the barn, now bumping together, now scattering into the field. Frank Charles keeps jerking and shouting, the dogs circle and growl and startle them at random, and sometimes the cows run in the direction of Alpo and sometimes they don't.

But once they do reach him, Alpo calms the cows into a trance and they don't move at all; they just stand there with blank looks while he does his thing. He makes notes on the small computer after examining each animal. When he's on the last few, and those are all corralled into a group, Claude opens the back gate of the truck and slides out a metal ramp. He climbs inside, grabs a long length of rope, and ties a loop in it. There's a bright flash in the distance and heavy thunder rolls in on the breeze. From up here he can see the long line of new thunderclouds coming in low over the endless stretch of stunted pine trees and scrub.

Back down in the field, he comes up on one of the white cows slowly, in the same way Alpo did, mumbling under his breath. He gets up next to it and lowers the rope over its head. He tightens it and gives a tug. The cow doesn't react. He tugs again, and the cow lifts its head and looks him in the eye. The cow's eye is dark brown and its iris is full and black like his father's, and there Claude is, alone in the middle of it all, reflected in that deep black pool of water.

The feeling passes. It's a cow, Claude tells himself. He gives it another tug and it starts walking with him, right up onto the back of the truck. In the cab, the flip phone is ringing, like some far-off, monstrous insect. He waits until it's done.

He's leaning over to untie the knot when he hears Alpo give out a kind of high-pitched keening, a weird sound, like a rabbit run over. Claude hops off the truck and comes around. "Fuck me!" Alpo yells. He's standing there in the center of a silent audience of cows with a gray look, holding one wet, gloveless, chimp hand up in front of his face and picking long slivers of a broken glass vial out of it. "The thunder spooked them," he says. "They all shifted. Goddamn it! Get me that gasoline, will you? This thing was full."

Claude brings a jug over and pours it. There are several shallow bleeding gashes across Alpo's small palm. Alpo grimaces as he scrubs his hand with the other gloved one, and nods for Claude to pour again. "I am so entirely fucked," Alpo says. "I mean, like entirely." He has Claude bring him a towel from the truck and he wraps it around the wound.

When they're finished loading, they douse the fly-covered, maggot-ridden bodies of the few dead cows with the rest of gasoline and set them alight. Alpo, subdued and withdrawn, has them toss in their gloves and masks and suits, and then he picks up another container of gas and spreads it across the field on the biggest piles of shit and sets them on fire too. They catch fast and burn high, and the black smoke is strong enough to make them all lightheaded as they lean up against the cab of the truck. The sky goes dark, and rain slides toward them in gray sheets across the trees.

Alpo hands Frank Charles a stack of twenties. "So you know where you've been, Frank?" he asks.

Frank nods and says, "I been down to the casinos in Folsom, drivin' all night. I got lucky at the craps there just like I do every couple months or so."

Alpo says, "And you're to wait four weeks before the milk is set for consumption or sale, as per your contract."

"I hear ya."

"Remember that consumption can have serious side effects, and that we can't be held liable in any way should you choose to ignore the guidelines."

"Yeah, yeah." He scratches at the dirt with his foot. First one, then the other. He says, "Hey, you guys ever think of doing chickens?"

"Chickens."

"Sure. Superchickens. Extra eggs, you know—maybe they could pop them out already hard-boiled." He cackles. "I mean, chickens are pretty bad to start with. You seen what they eat, how they live in those big farms? Eating shit all day, then they kill you. How much worse could it get?"

"I'll pass that along."

"You should. I'd never touch 'em myself, mind you. You know those things came from snakes?"

There's a bright flash and the slap of thunder and a cow from the back lets out a startled bawl. Frank Charles waves, though they're standing right in front of him, and he wanders back toward the house with the dogs in tow. The rain sweeps in like it was dumped out of a bucket.

Alpo and Claude get back into the cab of the truck with the heater on. Alpo sets the briefcase full of cow fluid behind his seat, sighs, and gestures toward the house. Frank Charles is out on the porch. He stands there with his dogs in a half circle around him and his face tilted up at the sky with a train of smoke blowing across him and the rain sweeping in, his arms outstretched like a preacher over his congregation.

"Guy's not right." Claude runs a hand through his hair to get it back out of his eyes. The bandages are soaked through with sweat and rain.

Alpo pushes the glasses back up his nose. "Can't say we didn't warn him." He lifts up his hand, peels off the towel, and studies it.

"So you've got to tell me," Claude says. "Is this all for real?"

Alpo looks over at him. "The supercows?" Alpo says. "Remember, you've only seen part of it. If this goes like the other test groups I've seen, within two weeks all of Frank Charles' livestock will be dead."

"Sure. Right." Claude looks out the window on his side. All of Frank Charles' cows have gathered under what's left of the barn. "What's that mean for you, then?" Meaning the scratches, his hand.

Alpo doesn't answer the question. "It's your last day, right?" Claude nods. "Roy-boy call you?"

"You know he did."

"He wants to make you an offer. You going to take it?"

"Should I?"

"I did." Alpo shakes his head, holds out the injured hand and gestures with it to take in the truck, the cows, the farm. "Learn from your elders. And kid? If you make the right choice—and I think you just might? Then the less you know about any of this situation, what's real, what's not, the better. Get me?"

Claude nods, feeling like he's swimming across the wicked current offshore of Bouctouche Harbor, struggling for shore. He reaches under the wheel and starts up the truck. He backs up to the barn to turn around, then pulls around the house. Frank Charles doesn't open his eyes, but he gives them two thumbs up as they pass. Claude pulls one short blast out of the air horn and there's a flash of lightning at the very same time. Frank Charles cracks one of the widest, most off-center grins Claude has ever seen. His long, piss-colored teeth jump out of the twilight, and his mouth and tongue are so deep and black that all the rest of that last drive—picking up cows, burning things—all the rest of his way back across half of the world to his father's Canadian coast in a beat-up old Dodge, all the rest of his long and quiet life spent catching fish and selling them to his father's cousins and their cousins and friends that he knew once as a child and would come to know again, the face ambushes Claude, jumping out of sets of double-yellow road lines when he least expects it.

THE BEEKEEPER OF RÍO MOMÓN

"WHAT YOU *DO*—" said the guy, and I rolled my eyes. He had on a red shirt and a Cleveland Indians baseball cap that I knew Hugo would think was ironic. "What you *do* is you go down to that burger cart. No, that one right there. *Sí?*" The guy pointed. Hugo nodded. It was across the flooded road, past the boys with the makeshift uniforms and the automatic rifles, past the tuk-tuks, down near where the bus was slowly being submerged. "*Doble hamburgesa con huevo.* You order the double burger with egg." He hitched up his beltless pants and put his hand on Hugo's shoulder—they were the best of friends now, apparently. "Then you sit on that bench. No, the blue one. Someone will come and get you." The guy kicked at one of the dark-haired kids who swirled around us, eyes wide, hands outstretched. The kid dodged easily, laughed, and made what I assumed was an obscene gesture with both hands.

"Can I eat the burger?" Hugo said. He mimed eating. "With egg? Can I eat it? Or will that throw off the signal?"

The guy blinked. "*Amigo,* it's your fucking burger, eh?"

"We don't want to buy drugs," I said.

"If we want to find Chuck, we need to think like Chuck, right?" Hugo said. "Chuck would *definitely* party with this guy, Kimmy."

I put my hand over Hugo's mouth. "We need to buy hammocks. *¿Hamaca?*" I drew a smile in the air with my hand. "*¿Amanka?* For the boat. For sleeping?"

"Oh," said the guy. He shrugged and looked at Hugo, who was, after all, the man. "Why didn't you say so?"

"I'm not *sure* why," I said, releasing Hugo to speak. "Why *didn't* we say so, Hugo?"

"A burger sounds pretty good right now is why," said Hugo. "*Hamburguesa*. With egg. Is it a chicken egg? *¿Huevo de pollo?*"

"*Gallina.*"

"What's a *gallina?*"

"The hen," I said. "The one that does all the work. Look, we really just want some hammocks."

"I take you to my brother's house," the guy said. "He has just what you want, *amiga.*"

"There's no one right around here who sells them?" I gestured vaguely. There were tents and ramshackle stalls at either end of the flooded street. People—gringos, mostly—sloshed slowly between them, heads down, with sodden bundles in their hands.

"My brother, he makes the *best* hammocks. For the sleeping. The very best." He signaled one of the tuk-tuk drivers. The driver started up his tiny engine and drove the rickshaw over to us through the flooded street.

"Of course he does," I said, shaking my head. I shifted my backpack. "This is going to take more than awhile, isn't it?"

"We got time," said Hugo. "Maybe we should eat first. I know this good burger place?"

I'd known Hugo since the third grade. If he had his way, we would have traveled here in search of Chuck powered solely by pot smoke and sugary breakfast cereals.

"Never mind," I said to the guy. "No thank you, *amigo*. Come on," I told Hugo.

"My brother, he will give you a very good price!" said the guy. "For the sleeping!" He climbed onto the step of the tuk-tuk. The driver followed slowly behind us as we waded down the sidewalk, through the crowds of children, away from the bus station and toward the stalls, or what was left of them. "What else you need? Fish? Bananas? Girls? You want to party?"

"Party?" said Hugo, turning back.

"Come *on*," I said, grabbing the frame of his pack and yanking it. Hugo stumbled and almost went down in the water, which was full of dirt and trash and a lot of other things that I didn't want to think about. The river and the rain together had dredged out all of the town's sins and were in the process spreading them around equitably. As if on cue, a pair of condoms swirled into the tiny eddy about my ankles. "This was a bad idea," I said, shaking my head. I was tired of the rain, the heat, of this country and all of the boys with guns. I was tired of traveling. The flight had been typically awful. The bus had been thirty-one hours of Spanish movies, rows of beautiful, terrible babies howling in chorus, roosters posturing and strutting down the aisles, and a goat bleating loud enough to raise the dead. I was tired of Hugo, all of his endless verbal banter, the ADD thing, the self-imposed frat-boy naiveté. I was tired of being tired. And I wanted a bath.

"Excuse me," I said to the tiny woman in the first stall. "Do you speak English? *¿Hablas español?* Awesome. *¿Has visto a este hombre?*" I held up the empty honey jar we'd carried with us since Lima—it had Chuck's self-portrait on the label next to an old tattooed Indian man, both of them in front of a line of hive boxes. But it was Chuck who stood out: his dreadlocked hair in supernova, his face in one of his characteristic amused grimaces. The old Indian guy just looked tired. These men, I thought, exhaust all of us.

The woman frowned as if her lack of recognition was a tragic source of grief to her. She shook her head silently. "*No lo conozco.*"

"Didn't think so," I said. "Well, hey, *estoy buscando hamacas?*"

"For the sleeping!" the woman said, suddenly electric. She threw her hands in the air and did a splashy little dance. "My brother's hammocks are the very best!"

"Of that," I said, "I have no doubt." I unzipped my money belt and watched as the crowds of children swarmed in for the kill.

« »

It had been nearly seven months to the day since I had heard from Charles Parham, aka Chuck Mustard, who we also called the Yeti for both his stature and his prodigious and elaborate white-blond hair. Chuck the squash farmer. Chuck the erratic scooter rider and crazed kombucha maker. Chuck the beekeeper and iconoclastic designer, whose bizarre and brilliant posters for our tiny urban farm in Oakland had gotten us noticed by Whole Foods and Trader Joe's and—disturbingly though very profitably—Walmart, and who I'd been more than a little in love with, though I'd been far from the only one.

Chuck Mustard, who had suddenly departed two years back, to travel South America on the strength of his expansive personality and a shoestring budget grant from Burners Without Borders to do some sort of economic development. (Though exactly where, how, and with what resources seemed highly uncertain and frankly a little suspect.)

Almost as soon as he'd left, his letters to me started to arrive about once a week, posted first from Baja and then Mexico City, and then from Belize and Managua and Panama, about a country a month. The envelopes were covered in bizarre stamps and Chuck's typical brand of exotica—Tolkienesque runes, diagrams that could have come out of Lovecraft, glorious people both living and elegantly dead, strangely beautiful alien landscapes in the center of which, of course, stood Chuck. Every inch of the page was covered in Chuck's calligraphic handwriting crammed in at different angles. There were sketches, too. Chuck's wiggling feet sticking out of a Mexican dumpster.

Chuck climbing a Mayan pyramid. Chuck in the back of a police car in handcuffs.

Hugo made fun of them at first, and I did too. It was hard not to. They were diary entries more than letters—who he'd talked with, what he ate (and how he'd gotten it), where he'd slept and with whom—the myopic musings of Chuck Mustard off in the third world, a self-styled modern-day Central American Kerouac. Hugo read them aloud sometimes in his best Beat poet voice and we'd laugh through a bottle of cheap organic wine.

After six months, even Hugo was hooked. And for me, it wasn't just that Chuck and I had worked side-by-side for so long, or that I had a thing for him; rather, Chuck's sincerity and his wide-eyed fascination with just about every detail of his journey pulled me in. He told a pretty good story too, it turned out—much better than Hugo. Both Hugo and I had our favorite scenes: Mine was the drunk Russian goth girl on the beach in Oaxaca; she pulled off Chuck's clothes and slapped him and then swam off into the ocean. Hugo's was the police raid on the drug dealer's party in Quito; Chuck had to jump out of a third-story window and hide in a dumpster with a tiny Chinese guy who made them both some tea afterward.

Every week for those two years, Hugo and I fell into this routine. I directed the volunteers and the daily orders. Hugo tended the livestock and struggled with his awful paintings. But then the letter would show up. We'd order Thai up to our apartment. We'd eat and drink too much. Despite my better judgment (and often to my perennial regret), Hugo would talk me out of my clothes yet again. And then, finally, we'd take turns reading.

Last we heard, Chuck was moving through Ecuador and down into Peru. It was kind of rough, he said, with all of the coke moving upriver from Brazil, and with problems between the Indians and Canadian oil companies. (*Canadians?* we wondered. *Really?*) But while his drawings showed boys playing with toy cars and real guns, soldiers carrying crates labeled "cocaina," and Indians coming out of the jungle with spears and bows, it didn't seem to faze Chuck much. He'd met someone, he wrote. (*And what else is new?* I thought.) He was heading out through the Amazon by boat. He'd decided to stay awhile at some Indian village and help them out with some beekeeping work.

And then, quite suddenly, the letters stopped.

What could I do? I sent out a search party, and that search party was us.

« »

Hammock hung, luggage stowed, I felt no better sitting up on the roof of the boat with the other poor, travelling gringos. Was it the lack of sleep or the chicken and rice on a wilted banana leaf? I couldn't tell. Everything had begun to shimmer. We passed through a bank of fog across the river, thick and hot and eerily silent, and when we emerged I saw us as one of Chuck's drawings: Hugo holding court in the flare of his borrowed joint, his face like a red mask. A woman, Hecuba, with tattoos and piercings, slept sitting up. Her tall Wiccan partner—a restless treelike woman, who crossed and uncrossed her legs. Keith, with the accent from Kentucky and the beard like a dead cat, cleaned a camera lens large enough to suggest significant over-compensation issues. One moment it was bright and very hot. The makeshift blue tarps flapped loudly and the wind blew dead smells up from the brown river. Then the next it was pitch black. Men were gambling and shouting two decks below. Someone turned up a radio for a minute and the heavy hip-hop drumbeats echoed off the bank and seemed to come from everywhere around us before it crackled and went quiet. Stars flared and vanished in cracks between the low, running clouds and from somewhere I smelled chocolate and sewage and something thick and flowery like the corpse of someone's grandmother.

"Are you OK?" Hugo asked, and I nodded, meaning no, I wasn't, not really.

"Thanks," I said.

"Because you look kind of not."

"Pray, continue," I said, waving my hands. "Bubbles. Multiverse. And, um, stuff."

"Sooo the question isn't whether we're alone," Hugo said, nodding. "The question becomes whether or not our universe is part of an inflating series of largely identical Hubble volumes, see, or is it more chaotic and subject to erratic formation of embryonic bubble-microverses?"

Hugo exhaled and gestured with his hands. "The implications, of course, are huge! If we believe in the mostly *identical* model, you could probably find a way to move from one universe to the next pretty easily—and, duh, most of those worlds would be pretty much like the one you're used to. A micro-bubble, however, could be an entirely different prospect. Then, all rules would be off! Everything you count on could change in a *heartbeat*."

You do too many drugs, I wanted to tell him. You are a bad painter and a mediocre farmer of pampered pigs.

Hecuba let out a prodigious snore. Hugo took it as encouragement and spun off in more random directions. I became convinced that there were no universes in which there would be a Hugo that that did not have an opinion on the vocal abilities of the Amazonian parrot and how that compared to the macaw across several parameters, including intelligence, playfulness and snugglability as a pet, as well as potential vocabulary, both speaking and understanding.

A spider jumped onto my shoulder. I twitched and brushed at it, only to find it was the long fingers of the tall Wiccan woman.

"You are seeking something, I think?" she said, in a lisping whisper. "Or someone, perhaps?" A silver pentagram swung in the deep hollow of her throat.

"Yes," Hugo called out in grand despair. "We're looking for our dead mother, lost in the jungle lo these many years!" He offered up his joint but the woman shook her head.

"Stop," I said. "We're really just looking for a friend of ours."

The woman studied us over her tiny spectacles with a knowing, self-important look. "I know this because I have a *gift*," she said. She tapped her temple.

"Let me guess," I said. "You can tell the future?"

"Kinda," she said. "But I also have the tequila." She held up a cheap pint. "For the drinking."

I reached out with both hands like a baby grabbing for a sippy cup. "You are my new best friend." The woman sat down and handed me the bottle. I helped myself. Her name was Sam, she said, and her wispy hair had mint woven into it.

"Your friend, he is in the jungle somewhere?"

"He's CIA," Hugo said. "He's embedded with the Indians. We're the backup."

"It's better if you just ignore him." I took the empty honey jar out of my bag and handed it to the woman along with a tiny flashlight. "Our friend Chuck was working with the Matses, we think."

"Did you know the Matses have this drug?" Hugo said. "They stake out this frog by its arms and legs, and then they scoop the poison off its back. Then they burn you and put the poison in your blister."

"That sounds unpleasant," Sam said.

Hugo nodded enthusiastically. "First you vomit," he said, tossing the remains of his joint over the side. "But then you see God. Well, demigods, at least. Demons. Talking jaguars and stuff."

Sam blinked and then nodded. She looked down at the jar and read the label. "So you're looking for the Río Momón," she said. She handed back the jar.

"Somewhere near it, yes."

"It is not so far from here." She reached for my hand and studied the palm. Then she leaned forward, shone the light into my face, and studied it intently. Her breath smelled like onions. She nodded, frowned, and then switched off the flashlight and handed it back.

"Will we find him?" Hugo said. "Or will he be lost forever in the humid darkness?"

"I hope you find someone soon," Sam said to me. "You might not know it yet, but you're pregnant, dearie."

"I'm . . ." I said. "Well." I looked at both of them for a long minute, and then my stomach turned over, and everything I'd eaten in the last twelve hours was in the hoodie in my lap. "Thanks," I said. I wiped my mouth. "I guess?"

Hugo stood up and flapped his hands. "I'll get . . . what? A towel?"

"Don't worry," Sam said. She reached out and smoothed some of the hair out of my sweaty face. "It can be a very beautiful time." She took away the tequila.

I counted back days in my head, tried to do some hormonal math, but it was beyond me. I folded the hoodie over on itself and set it down on the roof and then stood up. Hugo moved to take my arm with one of his looks, but I brushed him off. If she was right, he'd done enough already.

"I need the restroom," I said, and made my way down two decks, past where the soldiers and the oil-company people crouched around two big spotlights that they were shining onto the shore. There were several sweaty white boys in bad, bright clothes pointing and then a lot of sweaty Spanish boys with guns, working the lights. One of the older white boys looked me up and down curiously and offered me his rum. He had blonde hair plastered against his forehead and dots of perspiration formed where his moustache was starting to come in. I took a sip, and he said something suggestive in Spanish. I shook my head, patted him on his damp cheek and went past him.

I opened the restroom door, held my breath, stepped in. It was a tiny room with a hole in the spattered floor and a bare bulb swinging overhead. Through the hole I could see dark water rushing by. My stomach flipped again but there was nothing to bring up, so I folded myself into the cleanest corner and tried not to think about anything, which meant I ended up thinking about Chuck. The boat rocked and for a minute I felt myself falling across the surface of something. Was there a bubble universe where I'd just said yes and gone on his trip with him? *That* Kim would be a very different Kimiko from this one, raised in Cupertino by her thoughtful, hands-off parents. *This* Kim's rebellions were relatively tame (tattoo, degree in art history), and her adventures up until now (living in Oakland, running a farm) were small and distressingly normal. *That* Kim would have awesome dreadlocks of her own—black and tangled and commanding. She'd have anime tattoos up her back and out her arms and giant hoops through her ears.

I put my hand on my stomach but didn't feel anything. A mosquito landed on my bare knee and I watched as it leaned forward and painlessly inserted its proboscis. I didn't feel anything. Sometime later it pulled out and flew off into the night. I thought about that time I'd been out trying to get the new goats to breed. I hadn't thought it'd be a problem: Traalfaz, the black and white buck, usually had the opposite issue, mating with composters and spare tires and bales of hay, generally when I was giving a retailer tour. But this time he stared back at the doe and then at me with confusion in his devil-like eyes. *You could play him some James Brown*, Chuck said, coming up behind me. *Maybe he just needs a glass of wine*, I said. *Or some demonstration?* surprising myself. I'd been flirting heavily for weeks, with no luck. I didn't turn around, but sighed a little and leaned back against him. *Well, I don't have any wine . . .* Chuck said. Where had Hugo been? Somewhere off ruining another canvas. Chuck had slowly lifted up the back of my skirt and had run his damp, compost-covered hands all over my ass.

Someone knocked at the restroom door. I assumed it was the oil company boy, or even Hugo, and ignored it, but the knocking didn't stop. I stood and flung open the door to find Keith-the-Beard looking back at me. He took a step back. "Sorry!" he said. He waved his hands in front of him and backed away. "Sorry, little lady! Take all the time you need."

"It's all yours," I said. "Such as it is."

"I wouldn't want to miss more about the, uh, *mapinguari*. Is that what he called them?" He squinted an eye and shrugged in a what-the-fuck gesture. "You with that guy?"

"Oh fetid, one-eyed beast of legend," I said. "Only with knowledge can we expose thee!" He looked at me sideways. I tipped an imaginary hat to him.

Back on the roof, the sky had continued to clear but the air still felt heavy and wet. The river had narrowed, and the trees and vines had begun to reach out toward the boat. Hugo was in a debate with the women about the potency levels of foreign versus US domestic marijuana, a topic this time on which he actually might have been an expert. My hoodie lay just where I'd left it. I picked it up and carried it to the back of the boat and shook it out over the rail, but it slipped out of my hands. I didn't hear it hit the water, but after a moment I could see it floating downstream, arms outstretched, the UC Berkeley bear catching the light of the moon.

"Sorry," someone said. "About downstairs?" Keith-the-Beard appeared at my side. He offered me his flask; I took a swig and coughed. "Bubble-Up and Southern Comfort," Keith said. He nodded as if I'd said something. "I don't drink, but when I do it's the good stuff."

"That's . . ." I said. "That's just foul."

"I know, right?" He grinned, exposing stained teeth. He shifted the big camera around his neck and leaned on the rail. A cloud of bats flew over and off down the river. "You OK?" he said. "I mean, no offense? But you look . . ."

"I'm fine," I said. "I just need some sleep."

"Don't we all," he said. "Did you get a decent hammock? This guy at the station took me out to see his brother in the country. His hammocks were shit. I feel like I'm going to fall right through it. You think there's someone on the boat who might, um, share?" He squinted at me in a way that was meant to be a wink.

"For the sleeping?" I patted his arm on the rail. "If I find someone, I'll be sure to let you know." Someone tapped me on the shoulder. I straightened up and turned and saw Hugo, pointing toward shore, but then something smacked the side of my head.

For a second I thought he'd hit me, though that would have been very un-Hugo. But no, he was staring at me and whatever it was that flopped against the back of my neck.

"Dude," Hugo said, after a minute. "There's, um, a bat in your hair?"

I could feel the wings smacking against my shoulder and the tiny claws scrabbling against my scalp. Of course there was a bat in my hair. I jumped up and down and shook my head, but couldn't dislodge it.

"I thought that was like a myth," Hugo said, blinking and swaying on his feet. "That they got stuck like that?"

"Well it's not a fucking monkey back there!" I could feel the weight of it holding on. I looked at Keith and Hugo, who were both watching me hyperventilate.

"Did you know," Hugo said, "that there are more than nine hundred individual species of bats along this river, including an actual vampire bat?"

Reaching back with both hands, I got hold of something furred and paper-like and tossed it out over the water. The bat dipped, caught the wind, and was gone.

"Bloody hell!" called Hecuba across the roof. "You go, girl!"

"Did you want something?" I said to Hugo.

"Yeah," Hugo said. He pointed over the railing. "There's, like, an Indian?"

Over on the shore, spotlights from the lower deck had converged on a man. His face was painted bright red around his eyes and on his forehead and cheeks, and there was some sort of tattooing around his mouth that made him look like he had giant teeth. One hand held a spear. The other flipped us off. The boat turned toward shore and the engines cut, and there were angry shouts from down below. A radio crackled something urgent in Spanish that I couldn't catch.

I looked at Keith-the-Beard. "Did we have another stop?"

He shook his head. "Look, whatever happens, stay together, and stay with the boat."

"What do you mean, whatever happens?"

"I'm just saying." He frowned.

The boat bumped against the dock and a few boys jumped out to wrap the moldy hoops of rope around the pilings. Hecuba and Sam joined us at the rail. A few more boys jumped out with their guns held in the crooks of their arms and approached the Indian, who turned and ran up a path into the jungle. One boy shouted after him in Spanish, and then they all ran off into the jungle after him. More boys piled onto the dock and shone lights and shouted.

"Bloody drugs!" shouted Hecuba. "It's all these bloody drugs!" She pounded her fist on the rail, and tossed back the last slug of tequila.

"Quiet!" Keith-the-Beard hissed. He had angled his camera at the dock, and was trying to take pictures without anyone noticing.

"Fuck off, Yank!" She waved the empty bottle in his direction. Down below, one of the soldiers looked up at us and spoke into his radio. From the path came the sound of a shot. We all jumped. More soldiers and oil-company people ran up the path after the Indian. "Not good," said Hugo, shaking his head. "Those guns they have there? Those are definitely MGP-87s— those things pump out like eight hundred rounds a minute."

Keith-the-Beard looked skeptically at Hugo and frowned. Behind us, on the ladder, a soldier called out and gestured. "*Vengan por aquí,*" he said carefully, waving us over. He led us down a deck to the middle of the ship. "*Esperen aquí,*" he said, and pointed to a space between rows of oil-company crates. He mimed crouching down. The radio at his belt crackled, and he picked it up and spoke rapidly into it. Then he ran off toward the stairs, followed by more of the boys. Their footsteps thudded up the dock. From the jungle there was more shouting in Spanish and Quechua and then the boat was strangely quiet. I looked at Keith-the-Beard, who looked at Sam. Sam looked at Hugo, who said: "Did you know there are more than twenty different species of piranha, and that most of them are vegetarian?" Hecuba tipped the empty tequila bottle over her mouth, frowned, and then rolled it away down the deck.

"Stay here," Keith-the-Beard said. He stood up and adjusted something on his camera.

"Are you crazy?" I said. "And what happened to stay together?"

"Nothing, all right? Stay together. And stay here. I'll be back."

"You're going to . . . what?" said Hugo. "Take them all out with that lens?"

"If nobody finds out about this kind of stuff, then it's like it never happened."

"If you're not back in fifteen minutes, should we leave without you?" asked Hugo.

"If I'm not back in fifteen minutes, y'all could wait another goddamn fifteen minutes," Keith-the-Beard said. He peered up over the crates, and then crept around them and down the stairs. I heard him jump onto the dock, and saw his shadow run quickly up into the trees.

Kim sat back down. "And then there were four!" said Hugo in a deep movie-announcer's voice. "Dot dot dot."

I reached over and slapped him.

"What the hell?" He touched the side of his face.

"Just once," I hissed at him. "For just once, Hugo, can you fucking be serious for one time in your messed-up frat-boy listen-to-what-I-have-to-say-about-everything life?"

Hecuba made a quiet whistle, and Sam cleared her throat. Hugo looked away from me and studied the boards of the crate next to him. My stomach groaned and then everything was quiet. The boat bumped up against the dock. There were spiders all over the ceiling, but none of them moved, exactly— they just seemed to grow larger and shiver expectantly in place. A wet breeze blew down between the crates and stirred the hair on my forehead. I stood up and looked over the row of crates. The fat, broody moon was just starting to rise over the river. I sat down again. The empty tequila bottle rolled back down the deck toward us. Then the boat shifted and it rolled away and at the end of the line of crates a small brown hand on a brown arm reached out and picked it up.

"Bloody shite," whispered Hecuba. "Shite, shite."

"What is your problem?" said Hugo, and I elbowed him and then they all looked down to where another Indian was standing. Like the man on shore, his forehead and all around his eyes was painted bright red. He had dark hair cut straight across the brow, and tattooing that looked like stitches encircled his mouth and stretched back to his ears. He wore an oversize pink *Power Rangers* T-shirt, and in the hand that didn't hold the tequila bottle he held a large shotgun.

He stared at us for a moment. Then he tucked the bottle under his arm and held a finger to his lips. He turned and said something over his shoulder and two more Indians appeared behind him.

"If you say something about wabbit hunting, I will have them kill you," I whispered to Hugo.

Hugo opened and closed his mouth and then nodded. He had his hands up. So did Hecuba. There was a large splash on the far side of the boat, and I risked a look. A man who I assumed was the boat's pilot was swimming for the far shore.

"All hands abandon ship!" Hugo whispered.

But the Indians studied us for a minute and then moved quickly around the man with the shotgun to inspect the crates. More Indians came silently on board, some with painted faces and some without, and they began to pick up the oil-company crates and carry them down the stairs and out onto the docks, where other Indians appeared and hauled them off up a different path.

The whole process took place in complete silence. The man with the gun sniffed the mouth of the bottle, and then held it up in our direction with raised eyebrows.

"Dude, we're all out," Hugo said.

"Do they speak Spanish?" I said.

"Sometimes," Sam said. "Sometimes Quechua, too. *No tenemos más*," Sam said to the Indian. "*Lo siento.*"

"That's interesting," said Hecuba. "But are they going to fucking *kill* us?"

Sam shrugged. Around us the crates disappeared. The man frowned and tossed the bottle over the railing. Hecuba put her hands down. After a minute, Hugo did too. As the last crate was carried off, another Indian came up, this one wearing brown pants and a blue soccer jersey, and the two of them conferred. I couldn't make out any of it. Then the man looked at us and gestured toward the stairs.

"*¿Por favor, queremos quedarnos aquí?*" I said. "We want to stay on the boat." I pointed at the floor. "*En el barco.*" But the man gestured again, and the other Indian said something.

"I guess we need to go with them," Sam said. She and Hecuba exchanged a look.

"I told you this was a bad fucking idea," Hecuba said to Sam. "Didn't I? This whole bloody trip of yours."

"You did, dearie," Sam said sadly, taking her hand. "You did."

I looked over at the dock, but there was no sign of the other soldiers or Keith-the-Beard. Just a few Indians remained, watching us without expression. Some carried bows. All of the crates were gone. I sighed. Somewhere a monkey howled. What would Chuck have done in this sort of situation? Jumped into the river with the pilot? Fought off a cayman? Slept with an Indian woman with those tattoos around her mouth?

"Come on," I said, and took Hugo's hand. I led him down the stairs and out onto the dock, followed by the two Indian men. Once we were all off the boat, the other Indians on the dock undid the ropes and used a long pole to push the back end of it away from shore. The current caught it, and the boat slipped away and began to drift sluggishly downstream, turning in slow circles. In the moonlight it looked like a giant wedding cake, floating away out on the water. And then it went around a bend and was gone.

"Now that's encouraging," Hugo said. I took a deep breath. Hecuba's tattoos looked pale. We followed them up the path, the way the crates had gone. Hugo began to quietly classify the trees and plants by genus and species, and I nodded without actually listening. We walked for maybe five minutes until the path opened up into a small village: ten or so thatch-roofed huts crouched on stilts. The men pointed to one of the huts, and we went in. It was long, with a low roof and a floor made from what was probably bamboo, with compartments along the sides separated by hanging straw mats. All of the crates had been stacked down at the far end. It smelled of smoke and damp and cooking and sweat. There were families in here—women tending to fires, men and children eating. Some of the women were bare-breasted, and some had long palm whiskers piecing their noses and chins, and some of the older women and men had that same red paint across the upper half of the faces. The children wore shirts and shorts.

There was a larger sitting area on the far side, around another fire, and a woman gestured us over. Sam said something in Quechua to the woman, but she didn't seem to understand. We sat down.

"What exactly are we waiting for here?" Hecuba asked. We sat and watched the Indians watching us until they seemed to get bored and ignored us.

Hugo began to tell the story about how he'd been locked up in Chico on suspicion of grave robbing on Halloween. I stood up and walked down the length of the hut. I stopped beside a single older woman who was stirring a pot, and took the honey jar out of my bag. I held it up. "*Has visto a este hombre?*" I said, very slowly. I pointed to my eyes, and to the picture of Chuck on the label. "I'm sorry, I don't know how to say it in your language."

The woman smiled, squinted into my face and then squinted at the label.

"That guy with the big hair? You'll want to look out back," she said. She pointed out the rear door of the hut.

I blinked. "You speak English?"

"Kinda. I've only got a PhD in ethnolinguistics from Harvard. If you're expecting some sort of holistic, nature-based epiphany from a member of a mysterious primitive tribe, though, I may not be of much help. You'll be fine, by the way," she said, before I could ask. "Our fight is with the oil companies, not the trustafarians. They're probably texting for your Jeep as we speak."

"You," I said. "Um . . ." I felt dizzy.

"You kids are cute," she said. "Can I take my picture with you?" She held up a smartphone, stepped over, put her arm around my shoulder, and took a selfie of us. Then she patted me on the head and went back to her cooking.

"Out that way?" I said, and the woman nodded vaguely.

I went to the doorway. A path ran into the dark mass of trees. I looked back at the fire and saw the scene had turned homey. Sam and Hecuba were sharing a bowl of plantains. Some of the Indian children had gathered around Hugo, who was hamming it up. He stood and gesticulated, made deep voices, and ran in place like someone's dad. The kids all laughed.

I turned and went out into the dark. I felt my way down the path as my eyes adjusted to the moonlight. After a few minutes it curved to the left and opened up into an area that had been cleared of undergrowth. I remembered I had a flashlight and clicked it on. There were the hive boxes, stacked haphazardly around the clearing, but they were old and pretty beaten up. I opened the lid of one, and it was filled with the thick black webs of wax moths, like a beehive designed by H. R. Giger. If these were something Chuck had worked on, he'd been gone for some time. Off on the next adventure that was, in the end, all about Chuck.

There was a sound of running water from the other side of the clearing, and I decided that sitting by the water for a few minutes might be a good idea. I pushed through the trees and down a small hill, but my foot caught on something and I fell.

I threw out my hands and found myself up to my chin in mud at the side of a large pool. The moon came out, and I saw something moving toward me in the water, something large and white. I tried to pull myself out, but I was seriously stuck—when I pulled on one arm, the other sank deeper. The thing surfaced just in front of me and from the big round white face and the whiskers and those big round eyes that stared at me I was convinced for a second it *was* Chuck, after all. But then it belched, huffed air out of its big nostrils, submerged and moved slowly away from me, back into the pool, gone forever.

"Did you know," said Hugo from somewhere behind me, "that the Amazonian manatee replaces their teeth from the back to the front, kind of like a set of double conveyor belts? They can also control the flow of their blood to stay warm."

"I did not know that, Hugo," I said.

"Are you OK, Kimmy?" he asked. "'Cause, well . . .'"

"Yes," I said. "Yes, I'm definitely not OK."

"Do you need a hand?"

"Yes, Hugo. Yes, I think I do."

He pulled me out, and we sat at the edge of the mud. I put my muddy head down in his lap and imagined him as that bright little boy to whom everything came easy, the one I'd once stared at for weeks who sat in the back of the class with the huge plastic-framed glasses and those flashy Dungeons & Dragons books.

He took some of the mud out of my hair and then put his hand on my head. There was a South American fish that had a peculiar mating strategy, had I heard of it? Most of the little *poecilia parae* males were bright red and yellow, and they would compete for the female's attention, he said. But sometimes, while everyone was distracted, the smaller, less colorful males (who by the way had the larger testes) snuck up and did the dirty deed while no one was looking. And then that was that.

I turned my head and looked up at him. It was dark, so I couldn't see his face—all I could see was his silhouette looming low over me against the curved sky. The way the trees rose up behind his head made him look like he had these immense horns. He was silent for a minute in the way Hugo was never silent, and he started scraping roughly at the mud in my hair again. He pulled out a few drying clumps. His hand caught at something tangled there—a stick maybe. He tugged, harder than I expected, and it came loose painfully with some of my hair still attached to it. He tossed it into the water. A flicker of moon caught the white of his teeth.

I bit my lip and tried to catch my breath. Neither of us said anything. Somewhere, a parrot screamed. And then he took a deep breath and started again, on the topic of the virtues and dangers of the cryogenic storage of human heads; namely, that if you assume a world of ever-expanding population pillaged by dramatic income disparity and a crumbling slate of natural resources, most of which were by then underwater, where your home was a boat and your boat was a dinghy and the dinghy was sinking and there was nowhere to swim for food, why would anyone bother to bring back another frozen head to feed?

"But then again, what if? Hey, can't you see it, Kimmy?" He hefted my skull in his hands. "The two of our heads waking up together every day down on into the twenty-fourth-and-a-half century? What've we got to lose?"

"Nothing, Hugo," I lied, shivering there in the mud. I felt my stomach churn. "Nothing at all."

BIGFOOTS IN PARADISE

A S THE REST of them trudged over the rise, Brianna's girls flew on ahead, down the dry hill toward the campsite set back by the trees. They still had their monkey masks on, and the big dirty slippers with the furry brown feet and the stuffed claws. Suki trailed in their wake, saying *don't run, don't run!* and the girls listened to her as much as they did to anyone, especially Brianna, which was not at all. Zoey, the younger, pumped her arms to catch up to her older sister Lizzy, but tripped over a slipper and went down hard in a pile of tangled limbs. She rolled, churning up dust, and then sat up, mask askew, and she screamed a long list of curses at Lizzy's back. Then she burst into hot tears.

Suki reached her and knelt down, put a hand out in consolation. She remembered what it was like to always be trailing an older sister—her own had been *that* pretty girl, with the long flowing black hair, the perfect grades, the beautiful spinny skirt, while everyone had called Suki 'Little Mouse.'

But instead of taking Suki's offered hand, Zoey popped up on her toes and landed a small, hard fist square on Suki's cheekbone, just below her left eye. The blow knocked Suki back into the dirt. Zoey looked at Suki for a second, tiny shoulders tense, expression unreadable behind the mask: a little gorilla. Suki stared back at her in disbelief, her hand to her cheek. Then Zoey nodded, apparently satisfied, and turned and flew off again down the hill, high-stepping in her big furry feet Lizzy's pursuit.

Suki lay back in the dead grass and stared up at the sky. A turkey buzzard wobbled on a thermal way up there. Her cheek throbbed. She remembered a time that her sister caught Suki in her room, trying on her clothes. That withering look as she stood there, mortified to have been discovered, wearing Umi's too-big bra.

She wanted to have more sympathy for the little brat. But the kid sure didn't make it easy.

Hamsa came down, leaned over her and stuck out her tongue. Hamsa's eye makeup ran in sweaty black cascades down her cheeks, as though her eyes had struck oil in that dark place that was Hamsa's heart.

"Maybe we should have filmed that," Mike said, as the rest of them circled up wearily around her.

"Suki, that was great," Topher said. "Can you get them to do that one more time?"

With someone else, it would have been sarcastic. Suki raised the hand that wasn't covering her cheek to flip him off.

"I think that means no," Hamsa said, in a dry voice. "But I mean, I'm just guessing. What do you think, Bri?"

"I guess?" Brianna said. She shrugged and looked over at Topher for an answer, the way Suki knew Hamsa expected her to.

"Of *course* you do," Hamsa said.

"Hamsa," Topher said. "Would you just quit."

Suki sighed. It had been a long day of trudging, filming, and arguing. They had started off looking for places that met Topher's elaborate criteria as detailed in a lengthy email none of them had actually read:

> Topography is required to be both interesting and diverse without being too obviously staged or otherwise problematic. Locations can be neither too dark nor too bright, require a specific amount of undergrowth that is not too dense, nor too sparse, too green or brown, too leafy or spindly, too spiky or stark. Per Topher, a bigfoot in the classic tradition did not pose half-naked on boulders to show off his significant surfing-enhanced musculature, nor would he demonstrate a sophisticated level of technical rock-climbing acuity, despite Mike's suggestions to the contrary. A bigfoot, Topher wrote, shall be discovered seemingly at random, fleeing rapidly from the camera-holder through a mixed density of underbrush and filmed largely from behind, though periodic glimpses of the upper body and facial regions as the bigfoot turns and looks back at the camera holder will occasionally be acceptable if presented in the right context.

It took all morning.

Then there were the actual filming sessions themselves. Suki knew that Hamsa was a complete perfectionist at most things—they had been roommates for three semesters at UCSC, and where Suki's side of the room had always been a comfortable disaster, Hamsa's had been structured with her engineer's logic: clothes sorted by color and function, her toiletries and make-up (such as it was) in a row left-to-right in order of application. Given what had happened between her and Topher, Suki had expected Hamsa to blow off the videos. But instead, Hamsa took it to the other extreme and spent nearly an hour at each location to configure the drone, test the exposure on Topher's iPad, adjust the video filters, fiddle with the sound, and then re-check and adjust the settings while having them each stand in different points of the landscape while she flew the drone around them in slow circles. Then she'd move one of them three feet to one side and do it all over again.

As for the rest of them, Suki had called it all last night, sitting on her small porch and smoking by herself: Topher was more interested in running his fingers through his massive, carefully-cultivated beard and elaborating on the cryptozoological traditions behind each of his directorial "decisions" than actually getting much done. Hamsa's passive-aggressive micromanagement had Mike ready to kill. Mike was a smart guy but an awful actor, even if his job was simply running away from a camera in a gorilla mask. If he knew the camera was on him, he couldn't seem to help but stop and stretch and preen.

Suki had no idea if Topher had actually asked Brianna to bring the girls. On this, at least, everyone agreed: those girls were brats. Suki and Hamsa exchanged exasperated eye rolls when Brianna pulled up with them at the trailhead, flailing around unbuckled in the backseat of her shiny little Fiat. And when Brianna stepped out in her pig-tails and her cute little *My Neighbor Totoro* cape-hoodie, carrying her artisanal gluten-free vegan sandwiches in pretty boxes with ribbons, and then immediately clicked into a tight orbit around planet Topher, they both understood that as women together among young, Santa Cruz men of artistic aspirations, one of the two of them would also be expected to pick up Brianna's child-care slack in addition to doing much of the cooking and cleaning. And since Topher and Hamsa had split three months back when Topher had sent a sext of his hairy privates that he'd apparently intended just for Brianna to their own ongoing private group-text, Suki knew she was it.

Suki liked kids. She liked them a little too much, actually. Sometimes she would lie alone at night, in the loft bed in her tiny house tucked back behind the marijuana dispensary where she worked and think: she could put a fold-away crib there, next to the kitchen counter. A Pack'N Play could go over by the door. She would get one of those pouches you wear on your chest, and carry the kid around there like a little monkey. She'd be a much better parent than either of hers had been: Her mother, the original angry bigfoot, always loomed behind her. Her father was the invisible man.

Just not these two beasts. As predicted, the girls were a disaster, running off at random in any direction at high speed toward ravines and poison oak. And only Suki took off in pursuit.

But Topher had asked each of them to come. And just as Suki, Hamsa, and Mike had done in college and after—the awful spring break in Baja, that disaster with the organic farmers down near Big Sur, the time in Death Valley with those horrible mushrooms—they called in sick, they packed their backpacks, and they came.

Topher, Mike, and Brianna went on ahead, but Hamsa set down the drone, ditched her backpack and flopped down next to Suki. She pointed up to where a few more birds had joined the first one, circling awkwardly in the air overhead. "You think if we stay here and don't move, they'll come down?" she said.

"They can smell the dead a mile away," Suki said.

Hamsa leaned over and sniffed her. "Then that would be a yes."

"You shouldn't talk."

They lay on their backs, held still and watched. The birds drifted lower.

Suki closed her eyes. It was hot. She could see the whole list of camp set-up chores written there on the back of her eyelids with her name assigned to most of them. "Do you think bigfoots in the classical tradition would be capable of cooking dinner and cleaning up after themselves, just this one time?" Suki said.

"One can dream," Hamsa said. "One can dream."

Maybe she could sleep up here, Suki thought. Sure, it was a little rocky. But at least there was a view. She opened her eyes, and there was one of the turkey vultures, swooping down low, not five feet away. "Holy shit!" she said, and threw her arms up. "Shoo, shoo!" The bird startled back and flapped its big, black wings back up into the air.

She and Hamsa stared at each other, eyes wide. "That was…" Suki said, trying to catch her breath.

"Kind of awesome, in a creepy kind of way," Hamsa said, shaking her head. "Just don't tell Topher. He'd probably want to get that on camera too."

"Then he can have another word with my little friend," Suki said, staring down at her middle finger. This whole thing had been a bad idea from the start.

« »

The tents (Suki) were all up, the fire (Suki) was started, the food largely cooked (Suki, and, okay, some Hamsa too but mostly Suki), the craft beer (Mike, mostly) and local whiskey (Topher, of course) were at least half gone, and all Suki wanted was to stare into the flames and then drift off to sleep, but the incident with the bird had left her on edge.

And there was no getting rid of Brianna, apparently. "Are you sure? They're wheat-free." Brianna asked again. She held up the box in Suki's face. The ribbon was a perky neon blue, there in the firelight. "And artisanal!"

Suki avoided eye contact, a skill she had honed with the homeless in downtown Santa Cruz, and blew smoke out of the corner of her mouth. She'd apparently have to settle for getting stoned. Brianna frowned and coughed.

It was dark. The trees loomed over them. Something, Suki thought, was probably watching them. Hamsa handed the skewer she had been cooking to Suki and leaned over to spear a piece of raw chicken from a plastic bag with another stick. "Isn't 'artisanal' just another term for self-important white guys with beards on Instagram trying to get laid?" Hamsa said.

"Ouch," Mike said.

Brianna sighed. She looked uncertainly down at the box in her hands.

"Everything with you comes back to money and sex, Hamsa, doesn't it?" Topher said. He smoothed his beard down and then took a sip from a hip flask that was covered in pictures of gears, submarines, and squid. "I'll take one, Bri," he said.

"Everything with *me*?" Hamsa demanded.

Brianna skipped around the fire to Topher. "Take your pick!" she said, tugging on Topher's topknot.

Hamsa leaned forward. "I seem to recall *you* being the one with the search history full of fat cosplay girls in expensive tights."

"Here we go," Mike said. He leaned back in his camp chair and rubbed his hands together eagerly, looking over at Suki. "Again," he added. He opened another beer.

Suki sighed and blew smoke at Mike.

Brianna blinked. "Hey," she said, quietly. "I rock these tights."

"We all have needs, Hamsa," Topher said. "It's just that some of us find ways to get them taken care of, while others of us apparently expect to be catered to."

"I cater," Brianna said, looking around at all of them innocently. "I just don't do wheat."

"I'll bet you cater," Hamsa said.

Hamsa had told Suki she was sure that the whole thing between Topher and Brianna had started when Hamsa said she was tired of paying all of Topher's bills.

"Did you hear that?" Suki said. "I thought I heard voices." Or was it just a fox barking? They all stopped to listen. Brianna's two little girls giggled from off in their My Little Pony tent. A breeze moved through the trees. Nothing. And yet . . .

Once when they had all been hiking in Nisene Marks she had dropped behind to get a rock out of her sandal, and then she'd taken the wrong turn at a fork in the trail. She went down into a canyon where the coastal oaks tangled with each other and the sun came down through the canopy in columns. Everything was perfectly quiet. While chewing on a paleo energy bar she'd come across a mother boar with some piglets behind her, grunting softly and rummaging through the spiky oak leaves. She tried to be perfectly still. She watched as it dug up something with its snout and ate it and the piglets followed her lead, but when Suki reached in her pocket for her phone something shifted—some rocks dislodged and tumbled down from where she stood on the hill. The mother boar raised its head and saw her. It let out a shriek and feinted up at her. Suki, startled, fell backwards and sat down in the dirt. She heard the mother pig charging up the hill, and she covered her face and held out the paleo bar. She felt rather than saw the mother boar come up, sniff the bar and snort, and then they all ran off. When she'd looked up again, they were gone.

"Suuuuki," Mike said, stage-whispering with his mouth full. "Coooook meee more chiiiicken."

Topher laughed, but no one else did. Suki shook her head. Things were out there watching them. She heard the distant sound of a plane passing over. The longer she sat, the more she was sure of it. Were they speaking Spanish? Or maybe it was all just in her head. Were they the real bigfoots? The legend had to have been based on something. How was Mike like a real bigfoot? Suki thought. He was tall and kind of muscular. He shuffled his feet when he walked. He had big teeth. His skull was the size of a basketball. Mike chewed the organic, free-range bird with his mouth open, tasting nothing.

"Everything about *everything* comes back to money and sex, *I* think," Mike said. He still wore the gorilla mask, pushed back on his head. "I mean we wouldn't—"

"Nobody cares what you think, Mike," Suki said. She reached over and took Topher's shiny steampunk flask from his reluctant fingers and took a drink. The whiskey warmed her throat. She was exhausted and cold, and she shivered and hunched more into her warm Aztec poncho and tried to ignore that feeling in the back of her monkey-brain. Her face hurt from that bratty kid. She'd probably have a bruise. The last thing she wanted to hear was any more of Mike's voice. At least chasing after the kids had let her avoid him. She'd had such high hopes there last year. Mike had started going to the gym and had turned his thick, beer-drinking body into something very different. They'd been friends for a long time, and he was a smart guy, and she had always told herself there was something deeper to him than the superficial, sexist persona he put on in a group. He wasn't her type, really, but she made a bad call in a moment of weakness. Unfortunately, Mike was like one of the best-sellers she kept buying at the Santa Cruz Bookstore on Pacific Avenue. They looked good on display, but were disappointingly lacking when you took one to bed.

"I get that," said Mike, frowning. "I get that a lot. It's the price of being a true genius in my own time. But personally? I'd say artisanal *sex* is worth every single penny."

"You would," Suki spat. "And anyway, it's ar-*tees*-sonal." She took out another pre-rolled joint from her dispensary package and lit it.

"Like seasonal," Brianna chirped perkily.

"'Tis the *season* to get *busy*," Mike sang.

Topher raised his hand. "Isn't all sex ar-*tees*-sonal?"

"No," said Hamsa and Suki together, and they looked at each other. "No, it definitely isn't," Suki said, looking over at Mike. There were black flecks of meat in the gaps between his big, square teeth. She blinked her eyes rapidly, drew on the joint and blew smoke back over her shoulder. If she had had a baby with Mike, it probably would have been massive. Her stomach would have swelled up like she was having twins. The crib would have been the size of her house.

"Sing it, sister." Hamsa took her chicken out of the fire, examined it, and then stuck it back in.

"I guess you get what you pay for," Mike said. "Do we all think Brianna's enjoying herself? Well, do we?"

Brianna blushed and looked down at her hiking boots. Hamsa frowned and looked away.

Topher opened his mouth and then closed it. "All you people," he said. "It's been a long day."

"I thought we were just having a discussion," Hamsa said. "A simple discussion about overblown hipster egos."

"And sex," Mike agreed.

"And beards?" Brianna added, with a little clap. She looked around at all of them with big brown eyes as though pleased with herself for almost keeping up with the conversation. Had they been talking about beards? Suki thought. No, they had not.

"Do not meddle in the affairs of beards," Mike said, ominously. "For they are smelly and quick to lecture."

"Hah," said Hamsa. "Hah!"

Topher grimaced at Mike. Mike shrugged an apology. Maybe Topher didn't actually realize that when he hiked, there was this funky ghost of him that trailed just downwind, a grody shadow? How was Topher like a bigfoot? Suki thought. That was easy. He was hairy. He smelled bad. He wandered through his life in Santa Cruz seemingly at random, foraging for sustenance and sex. In general Topher respected Mike—Mike was smart, but also took direction well. When they played together on Pacific Avenue in Santa Cruz, it was Mike who played that big bass drum that kept everyone on time. It let Topher jam and improvise on his shiny new ashikos and really stand out, and Suki knew Topher liked that. Maybe they'd be bigfoot bros together, high-fiving and backslapping their way through a sort of consequence-free hipster paradise.

"Did you hear that?" Suki said. Everyone went quiet. Sparks lifted up and scattered away from them, up into the air where they turned into unfamiliar, flickering stars. Somewhere a coyote barked. A bat winged over their heads, high and erratic. "I thought I heard something moving in the bushes," Suki said. She was sure this time.

"Again?" said Topher.

"Again," said Hamsa.

"Spooooky," Mike said. "That's what you get for not sharing the pot."

Suki gave Mike the finger, right up in his face. He pretended to bite at it. She left her finger there and it ended up in his mouth for a minute and both of them looked startled. Suki blushed. She took her hand back. The smoke from her joint drifted past Topher, who coughed and waved his hands in front of his face. "Well, if I wasn't hungry before, I sure am now," he said.

"It's organic," Suki said.

"Hungry for what, exactly?" Hamsa said. She took the piece of chicken out of the fire. It was done perfectly even on all sides, just the right shade of brown without being burnt or undercooked. She devoured it.

"*Moving.* In Brianna's *bushes*," Mike said. "Heh."

"Does *anyone* want to try a sandwich?" Brianna asked, in a small voice. The box still sat by the side of Topher's chair, untouched.

"They're *artisanal*," said Hamsa and Mike at the same time. Mike snickered.

Brianna frowned. She pulled the head of the Totoro hoodie closer around her face. The creature's ears looked deflated, the big wide grin forced and sad.

"You know, you are kind of a cretin," Topher said to Mike, after a minute.

Mike nodded and stood up. "I am hugely cretinous!" he shouted. "I am a beast of awesomely epic proportions!" He thumped his broad surfer chest hard with two large fists and howled like a wolf. The gorilla mask slid off the back of his head. Then he stumbled backwards and sat down hard, just missing the drone.

"You are also hugely drunk," Hamsa said.

"Maybe he needs to do *that* in the video," Suki said.

"Get drunk?" Hamsa said. "'Cause we all know that's not a problem for him. By the way," Hamsa gestured with her skewer. "I think that's poison oak."

Mike lay back on the ground in the leaves. "Do you want to come over and scratch me?"

"Maybe," Hamsa said thoughtfully, looking at Topher. "Maybe I do."

"I thinks I really needs me a scratching," Mike said. "Grrr."

"I meant the howl," said Suki, sighing dramatically.

Topher looked at her across the fire. Hamsa looked back. Suki knew what Hamsa was doing, using Mike to bait Topher. If the last few years were any example, it would work. Hamsa had confessed to her while they were walking: if she was honest, she missed those weekend mornings, waking up in the drafty Santa Cruz Mountain cabin all tangled up in Topher's hair and gangly limbs, knowing that perfect pour-over coffee was just a few steps away. Hamsa would extricate herself and come back with steaming mugs. Topher would slowly come awake and tell her about all the brilliant ideas he'd had overnight, all the possible futures they could choose to explore, there among all the redwoods. It had been a paradise, of a sort. If only there hadn't been that tacit, open relationship with Hamsa's bank account. (And that hi-res picture of his dick.)

"I'm not sure a classic bigfoot howls," Topher said, after another minute of staring at them all. "The standard expectation of a bipedal vocalization is more of a roar."

"Grrr?" said Mike again, hopefully.

"I hope the girls don't itch tomorrow," Brianna said, looking pointedly at Suki. "They were in the bushes a lot and Lizzy is very sensitive to poison oak."

Suki opened and closed her mouth. A bigfoot would be a far better parent than Brianna, she thought. A mama-bigfoot would have her for breakfast.

The burning wood popped and shifted. A light breeze came through again and brought in the salt of the distant ocean, and the redwoods groaned to each other. Off in the tent, the girls were arguing. Suki was sure she heard other voices now, coming in on the wind. Were they speaking Spanish? Two or three of them—what were they saying? And there was that bat again. It swooped down low over their heads, and Suki imagined for a minute the bat was her. She was flying off, away from here. She'd find an old vineyard to roost in, one where she could hang safe, upside-down from the vines, and eat ripening grapes one at a time. Was that something looking at them from between the trees? A face, she was sure: dark skinned, black hair! She was about to stand and point, but then the fire popped and the light shifted. A shadow, and then: nothing.

"Should we actually be having a fire?" Brianna said to no one in particular. "I mean, we might get in trouble?"

"It's a *fire ring*," Mike said, sitting up. "Why put it there if we're not supposed to use it? You know, the whole coastal ecosystem was built up around regular fires before people even got here! The Chumash used to set huge fires to scare out the wildlife for their hunts. If you really want to go back to nature— real nature—I say burn the whole mountain down!" He looked around at them and nodded convincingly to himself.

"Only, I'm not so sure that's true," Suki said.

"Pretty sure it's not," Hamsa said. "But yay you for going for it there, all on your very own."

"But what about the footage? Bigfoots fleeing from a forest fire? I mean, that would be fucking awesome, wouldn't it?" Mike said, laying back and gesturing dramatically with his arms in the air.

Topher combed his beard with his fingers. "I haven't seen anything like it," he admitted.

"No," said Hamsa. "Just, no. We're not burning down the forest for your fake bigfoot video."

"Yeah," said Brianna. "Maybe not the best idea. But I'm sure you'll think of another one." She leaned in closer against Topher, almost tipping him over in his tiny camp chair.

"Watch out for all those sandwiches," Hamsa said. "Wouldn't want them to get, I don't know, smashed or anything."

"Did you know they're wheat-free?" Mike asked.

"I did not know that," said Hamsa. "And vegan too? Be still my heart."

Brianna put her face down in her hands, which were round and kind of dirty. Topher stood up and scowled at all of them. "Fuck you," he said. "Fuck all of you. Just leave her alone."

Hamsa would make a good bigfoot, Suki thought. She'd wear the perfect flowers in her fur. She'd have the world's most organized cave.

It was quiet for a minute. There was the sound of a hiss, a tiny squeal—like an owl swooping down on a rat.

"So . . ." Mike said, attempting to change the subject. "Did we actually get anything good?" He pointed with his beer bottle at Topher's backpack, which held the iPad.

Topher sighed and nodded. "I think so." He took out the iPad, sat down and opened up the video app. He tapped it a few times, turned it around and hit the play button. It was a blurred video where the camera moved fast through the woods, and then it came up over the edge of a dry stream bed. Down in that rocky ditch were Mike and the girls in their masks and claws and slippers. As the camera came over them, they pretended to startle, and then scurried up the rocks on the far side. Mike turned and looked back and shook a furry fist at the camera.

Suki could see the story playing out in Topher's head: the video, he was sure, would be seen worldwide. Tens of thousands of views the first week of posting alone. It would be relinked and retweeted, picked up by major crypto-news sites, even made part of Discovery channel programs. Then he'd produce a whole series of flashy cryptozoological videos. Yetis in the Himalayas. Diving in Loch Ness. Probably no one else was making them. But if they were, they definitely wouldn't make them with his consistency with the canon, with his level of superior quality or his intense attention to every production detail.

Suki thought it looked pretty bad.

"Don't the girls look cute?" Brianna said.

"Would a *classic* bigfoot shake his fist?" Hamsa said. "Is that consistent with the prevailing cryptozoological fake-video paradigms? I mean, I'm just asking."

"Good point," Topher said. He ran his fingers through his beard. "Good point."

"You know," Suki suddenly announced, "I think we're all bigfoots!" It felt important, somehow, to say it—all of them there, around the fire in the middle of nowhere, with those towering trees looming and the darkness just barely held back by the firelight. "All of us!"

"Bigfeet?" Mike said.

"No, *really*." Suki leaned forward and gestured in the air. She was stoned, very stoned, and frustrated by her lack of ability to communicate what she was feeling. She ticked things off on her fingers. "We're all lonely. We all have our secrets. We're all running and hiding from something, right?"

Brianna looked back at her. Her lips were pursed, her brow was deeply furrowed. She nodded somberly. "I get you, sister."

"I've got something we could hide together again if you want to," Mike said.

"That's just so *profound*, Suki," Hamsa said. "Maybe we should hug and enjoy our epic connection with the Gaia spirit."

"Why are we all here?" Mike said to the sky. "What's the meaning of life? Is the truth really out there?"

Suki looked around at all of them. "Never mind," she said, deflated. "Never fucking mind." How was she like a bigfoot? She wasn't like a bigfoot at all. She sat back and burrowed back into the shawl. She could feel the rubber mask, cold and flaccid in her big double-pocket.

"I think you're all monsters," Brianna said quietly. She looked over their heads, out into the trees.

"Grrr," said Mike, from his bed in the poison oak.

"So what did you guys think?" said Topher. "I mean, really."

"How is this thing going to bring more people into the museum, again?" Suki said. Suki knew that while Topher "worked" at the Bigfoot Museum in Felton, without Hamsa it was now his parents who paid for his apartment, his fully-renovated Volkswagen van, his iPad, his many drums, his expensive bourbon and his hopelessly rotating ambitions. "Maybe I should have asked that ahead of time."

"All that hair feels a little derivative of a certain picture that turned up on my phone recently," Hamsa said.

"What picture?" Brianna asked, suddenly suspicious.

"It's nothing," Topher said, quickly.

"You didn't tell her?" Hamsa said. "You should probably tell her."

"She means his dick," Mike said.

Hamsa looked at Brianna and shrugged, faux-innocently. Then she uncoiled herself from her camp chair, went around to Mike and offered him a high-five. Mike took it, but then grabbed her hand and pulled Hamsa down on top of him.

"Eeew," Hamsa said, pushing up off his chest with both hands. "You smell like chicken."

"I taste like chicken, too," Mike said.

"I think I'm going to be sick," Brianna said. She glared at Topher, who looked away, and then she looked at Suki for some sort of sympathy. Suki smiled back vaguely and thought *you are a bad mother and you dress like a little kid. Also you apparently make really poor choices about sex.*

"You know, if you put your hand here," Mike said, reaching down to his crotch, "I will quack like a duck."

"Pass," Hamsa said. Though she settled herself in on his lap. Topher glared at both of them.

Mike shrugged. "Life is hard when you're made of meat." He scratched at a spot on his arm.

The noises again, for sure: Suki heard something large, moving in the leaves; the crack of branches. Why was no one else hearing them? "Did you hear that?" Suki said. She stood up and gestured to all of them. "Shhh!"

"Oh my god, Suki, stop!" said Hamsa. "Just stop it!" She whispered something to Mike, and he guffawed.

"Maybe the truth *is* out there!" Mike said.

"No, really! Maybe it's a mountain lion!"

They all listened. It was completely silent, but then the bushes back behind where Suki had been sitting began to sway and thrash.

Suki jumped to her feet and backed away, stepping on the boxes of sandwiches. Hamsa sat up with her hand over her mouth.

Then Brianna's two girls jumped out of the bushes wearing their masks, with their hands held high over their heads. "Boo!" they shouted, "Super boo!" They ran screaming in circles around the fire. Topher startled and tipped over backwards in his tiny chair.

"Giiirls," Brianna said, in a forced, light voice. "Girls, it's waaay past your bedtime now, isn't it?"

"*Giiirls*," mocked Lizzy, who was seven. "It's fucking *time for bed*!" She shook her fist at Brianna and then flipped her off. Then Lizzy yanked the iPad out of Topher's surprised hands while Zoey grabbed the drone, and the two girls ran off with the equipment into the woods.

"Fuck!" sighed Topher, on his back. "All of our footage is on that!" He threw his hands up in the air and let them fall.

"I guess we should go get them," Brianna sighed, looking dejectedly at Suki. By "we" Suki knew who Brianna meant. "They're going to get lost again."

"Yes," said Suki. "Yes, we should. Except I am not actually the mommy here." She sat down again and stared pointedly at the fire. Maybe the girls would use the iPad to find a new parent, Suki thought. Was there an app for that?

Brianna stood up and looked at Suki. Suki stared back at her. Brianna huffed and put her hands on her hips. She looked at Topher, who continued to lie on his back. He stared up at the sky for a long minute. Then he groaned and closed his eyes. "I give up," he said.

"Quick, more whiskey," Hamsa said. "Maybe that will help."

Brianna looked around at the rest of them. The fire was low.

Hamsa had sat back down in Mike's lap and was fiddling with a lock of his hair. "Grrr," Hamsa said quietly, looking over at Topher.

"It's not really that dark," Brianna said to no one. "I guess." She stood in front of Topher for a long second with her shoulders low. Then she went over to stand in front of Suki. She moved one foot back and forth in the dust. "It's not really that dark, Suki."

"Oh, fuck," said Suki. She stood up and went over to Topher and kicked him. "If I'm going, you are too." Topher groaned but did not open his eyes, so she kicked him again. "Rise up, Mr. Beard. Walk the earth once more."

Topher protested again, but then rolled over and climbed slowly to his feet. "Does anyone have a flashlight?" No one did. Topher sighed loudly, and stuck his hands deep in the pockets of his skinny jeans. Suki gestured to Brianna to go first, into the woods, but Brianna pulled the furry hood closer around her, crossed her arms over her chest and looked fearfully out into the trees.

Suki threw up her hands and struck out away from the fire. She kept her arms out in front of her and walked slowly in the direction she thought the girls had gone, feeling ahead of her with her feet. She couldn't see anything, but then her eyes started to adjust, and she could at least see the bigger roots ahead and keep from stubbing her toes too badly. Trees loomed up at her out of the dark. "Lizzy?" she called. "Zoey?" She kept walking in what she hoped was a mostly straight line until she walked into a tree and cursed. She stepped around it, saw a faint trail, and followed it. She could smell the ocean. She could hear Brianna and Topher arguing back there in the trees; Topher's low conciliatory voice, Brianna cursing and crying.

Ahead of her, then: a scream! A girl's scream, she was sure, and then shouting in Spanish. The moon was coming up, and as she came up over a rise she saw Lizzy tearing up the hill towards her, with Zoey just behind, and several men were in pursuit, flashlights swinging wildly, about a hundred yards behind them. The men wore dirty white T-shirts & cargo shorts, baseball caps on backwards. One of them carried the broken remains of the drone—it slapped against his legs as he ran. Another had a shotgun that he stopped and fired off into the air—the sound made her jump.

Beyond them, where the path opened up and the trees fell away into a field, she could see scattered trash, bleach containers, irrigation lines, and then what were probably marijuana plants: hundreds of them all in rows, an illegal grow.

Suki ducked back behind a tree. She felt her chest go tight, her stomach drop, her pulse suddenly pound in her temples. What would a bigfoot do, she wondered? She felt the mask in her pocket. A bigfoot would stand up a roar. It would fall down on those men like a demon. They would all stagger backwards, jaws dropping, and they would run.

Lizzy ran past her. Suki reached out, grabbed her, and pulled her in tight. Lizzy kicked and squirmed until she saw it was Suki. Then Zoey ran past them, gasping and sobbing. Suki grabbed Zoey's hand. The kids' eyes were wild; their chests were pounding, and their noses running with snot. "Come on," she hissed. "Come on!" She led them off the path, into the woods. They ran between the trees until they found a dry stream bed, filled up with old branches and sharp pin-oak leaves. "Down here," Suki said, spotting something. It was a lean-to of sorts, a lot of redwood limbs tangled together, covered over with a lot of leaves. "Quiet," she said. "Don't say a thing," and in the darkness she sensed rather than saw both of the girls nodding. They climbed underneath the branches, and she lay back against the dirt. Both of the girls curled tight into her, one on each side.

Maybe this is what a real bigfoot would do? Suki thought. Run. Hide. Zoey shook with silent sobs. Suki could hear the shouting, a little more distant than before. Another gunshot. Should she warn the others, around the fire? She knew she should. And maybe she would, in a few minutes. But for the moment, she'd lie here, quiet in her cave, and feel the girls' heartbeats pounding through their tiny little bodies, feel their hot breaths against her neck.

Doug Lawson's fiction has been cited as a 2014 Distinguished Story by the Best American Short Stories anthology, received an Honorable Mention from the O. Henry Awards, and has appeared in a number of literary publications, including multiple times in *Glimmer Train Stories* and the *Mississippi Review*, as well as in *Passages North*, the *Sycamore Review*, and others. He's won *Glimmer Train's* yearly Fiction Open, received a Transatlantic Review Award for fiction, a Henfield award, and a fellowship from the Virginia Foundation for the Humanities.

Doug lives in Charlottesville, Virginia, and the Santa Cruz Mountains in California.

His blog is online at HouseOnBearMountain.com.